Nicole O'Dell

ALL THAT GLITTERS

Interactive Fiction for Girls

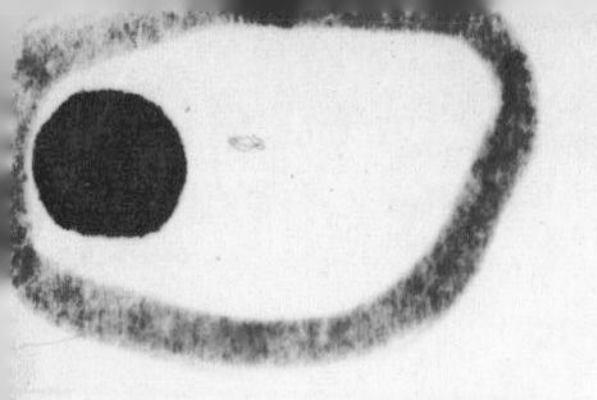

ISBN 978-1-60260-400-1

Published by Barbour Publishing, Inc., P.O. Box 719, Uhrichsville, Ohio 44683, www.barbourbooks.com

Our mission is to publish and distribute inspirational products offering exceptional value and biblical encouragement to the masses.

Printed in the United States of America.

Nicole O'Dell

ALL THAT GLITTERS

Interactive Fiction for Girls

Look for more scenarios books

Magna
and
Making Waves

Coming soon to a bookstore near you.

This book is dedicated to my daughters,
Natalie and Emily. Your sweet spirits and love for Jesus
inspire me to live my own life of faith. I pray that this series
of books will help you plan ahead and make commitments
about the choices you will face. I'm so proud of you both,
and I love you more than you could ever know.
—Mom

Chapter 1

TIME FOR A CHANGE

A fancy sports car on one side and a shiny, brand-new SUV on the other, Mrs. Daniels slid her car into a parking spot at the mall. More than any other year, shopping for school clothes this year was a very important task. Dani and Drew, identical twins, were starting the ninth grade—freshman year, the first year of high school. They knew full well how important their first impression was—well, at least Drew did. She had spent most of her summer planning and researching fashion trends, hairstyles, and makeup tips by reading fashion magazines. Not that it would do her much good, she often thought. Their parents didn't allow them to wear makeup; and her long, straight, dark hair looked just like her sister's and was cut and styled in the same style they had always had.

"Mom, I think it's time for a change," Drew announced as they walked through the parking lot toward the mall.

"What kind of change?" Mrs. Daniels asked hesitantly.

"You know, change isn't always a bad thing." Drew thought her mom might need some convincing before she tried to state her case. "Change can just be a part of growing up and a sign that a girl is secure and comfortable with herself."

"Yes, Drew, I'm aware of that. Why do I have a feeling that I'm not going to like what you're about to suggest?" Mrs. Daniels sighed good-naturedly and looked at Drew's sister, who shrugged her shoulders, not knowing anything about the big change that her twin was proposing. "Well, let's have it. What have you got cooked up?"

"Oh, it's really not a big deal, Mom. I'd just like to get my hair cut." Drew pulled a picture of a hairstyle out of her pocket and showed it to her mom.

Mrs. Daniels could see immediately that

the softly layered style would cascade to a very flattering place just below Drew's shoulders. She looked at Dani and raised her eyebrows. "Do you want your hair cut like that?"

"No, Mom, you don't understand," Drew interrupted with a slight whine, nervous that she wasn't getting her point across. "If Dani cuts her hair like that too, then I don't want to. This is how *I* want to look. . .by myself. I want to make a change, even just a slight one like my hairstyle, to separate myself from just being 'one of the twins.' I want to be an individual; I want to be Drew."

"Ah, I see, now." Mrs. Daniels had always known that this would happen one day and, she had to admit, high school was a reasonable time for it to occur. It pained her to think of her baby girls reaching such an independent place, though. "How do you feel about that, Dani?"

"Well, to be honest, I really don't want to change my hair. And I like being 'one of the twins' as Drew put it. I guess I don't see how that's a bad thing. Why would changing your hair to look like a picture of someone else make you an individual anyway?" she asked pointedly, turning to Drew.

"It just gives me the chance to express

myself and be different than I have been."

"As long as you really mean 'different than you have been' and not just that you want to be different than me." Dani tried not to be hurt, but it was difficult.

"Aw, sis, I love you. Nothing can change that we're twins. That will always be a part of us. We're just talking about a haircut here."

"I guess you're right." Dani laughed. "Let's go get your hair cut so we can all get used to it while we try on clothes."

First stop: Shear Expressions for a new hairstyle. Luckily, there was no one ahead of her, because Drew was too excited and impatient to wait. She took her seat in the shampoo chair, and the stylist began to lather up her hair. After the shampooing was finished, she patted Drew's head dry and moved her to the station where she would be cutting her hair.

Drew struggled to get her hand into the front pocket of her jeans so she could show the stylist the picture of the haircut that she wanted. "Um, Drew, I didn't realize that your jeans were getting so tight. We're going to have to be sure to buy some new jeans today."

"*Mom.*" Drew laughed. "This is how I

bought them. I want them this way."

Mrs. Daniels looked at the stylist, obviously a mom herself, and shrugged her shoulders. "I know," the stylist said, "it looks uncomfortable to me, too."

"This is what I want." Drew showed her the picture, ignoring the comments about her jeans.

"Oh, that's going to be easy enough and beautiful, too. We'll just take this hair of yours and cut some layers into it. We'll probably need to take off about three inches, but you have plenty of length so it won't even be that noticeable. Are you doing the same cut?" The stylist turned to Dani.

"Nope, not me. I'm staying just like this."

"All right then, let's get started."

Thirty minutes later, with dark hair in little piles all over the floor around her, Drew was staring into the mirror in front of her, getting her first look at her new self. She was stunned by what she saw. After looking at her sister for so many years, she was used to having a walking mirror right beside her. But now, as they both gazed into the mirror and took in the changes, they realized that a simple thing like a haircut signaled major changes afoot. Dani was sad when she saw the differences between them, but Drew was thrilled with her new look.

"I *love* it!" She spun around to the right and then to the left and watched her hair bounce in waves around her shoulders. "It moves, and it's free." She didn't miss the long, thick straight locks a bit. "It has personality. Thank you so much. You did a perfect job," she said to the hairdresser.

"I'm so glad you like it. I think it looks great, too." Both the hairdresser and Mrs. Daniels were a bit more reserved out of sensitivity to Dani.

"Mom, what about you? Do you like it?"

"You look beautiful, dear. Very grown-up."

"Now I'm ready to shop." Nothing was going to contain Drew's excitement as they left the salon; she was thrilled.

"We need to be wise now, girls. There is a limit to today's budget. My question is whether you want to split the budget and each get your own clothes—or do you want to pick things out to share and get more that way?"

Drew was trying to be more of an individual, but even she could see the logic behind pooling their resources and sharing the clothing allowance; and she knew that Dani would agree. But Drew did have one trick up her sleeve that she decided to save for later in the day.

They spent the day trying on clothes. It helped that both girls were exactly the same size and basically liked similar things. By the end of the day, they had successfully managed to supply their wardrobe with all of the basics they would need for ninth grade, including new winter jackets, jeans, tops, sweaters, belts, socks, pajamas, undergarments, accessories, and shoes. They were exhausted by the end of the shopping trip, and Mrs. Daniels was more than ready to go home.

As they were walking toward the exit door, Drew said, "Mom, you mentioned that you have grocery shopping to do. Would it be all right if Dani and I stay here and meet up with you when you're finished? I have a few things I still want to look for."

"I suppose that would be okay, but I'm done with dishing out money today. So what are you looking for, and what will you do once you find it?" Mrs. Daniels laughed.

"I brought some of the money I saved from babysitting this summer, and I really want to use some of it to get a few unique shirts or something that will be just mine—you know, signature pieces. I promise I won't spend it all, Mom."

"Oh, I see. This is part of your search for individuality? Is that it?" At Drew's nod, she continued, "I don't see anything wrong with that. But, Drew, just remember what your dad and I allow and how we expect you to dress. No supertight jeans, no shirts that show your belly, nothing with a saying or advertisement that your dad and I would find inappropriate. Think of it this way: nothing that I wouldn't let you wear to youth group. Deal?"

"Got it, Mom. Thanks, you're the best."

After they discussed their meeting time and location, Mrs. Daniels left the girls to their shopping. Dani wasn't too happy about it, though. "Why couldn't you have done this while we were shopping earlier?" she asked Drew.

"Because I wanted to finish the shopping for our stuff and then I would know what I still needed."

"Oh, sis, there's nothing else that you *need*."

"I know, that's what makes this part so fun. It's all about what I *want*."

Dani sighed and suggested they get started before they ran out of time. With her own money, Drew selected two snug plaid shirts to wear over a tight black T-shirt that she found. The flannel shirts barely reached her waistband, but the T-shirt was long enough, so she thought it would pass. She also selected a cropped denim jacket that was covered in studded rhinestones. Dani liked the jacket, but it wasn't really her style at all. Drew also picked a few cropped sweaters that, if worn alone, would be way too short for her mom's approval, but with a T-shirt or tank underneath, would probably get by. Her favorite and most expensive purchase was a black leather belt with a big silver buckle covered in rhinestones in the shape of a big rose. Drew thought that it was unique enough to become her signature piece.

"Well, one thing you won't have to worry about," Dani assured her, "is me bugging you to borrow any of the things you bought. They're all yours."

Their time was up so they hurried to the exit door to find Mrs. Daniels already waiting there for them. As they slipped into the car, she asked, "Well, was your search successful?"

"Oh, yeah! Mom, I found some really cute things," the ever-excited Drew told her mom.

"Yeah, real cute," Dani said, rolling her eyes.

Sensing from Dani's reaction that there might be something she needed to see in those bags, Mrs. Daniels said, "Great. Then we can have our own private fashion show when we get home."

"Sure, Mom. No problem."

After dinner, Mrs. Daniels remembered that she hadn't checked out Drew's purchases yet. "Drew, why don't you get those things that you bought so we can make sure that everything is acceptable for you to wear."

"Mom, I know the rules and I followed them. I don't see what the concern is."

"There's no real concern, honey; but I'd appreciate if you don't argue with me and just humor me. I am only looking out for your best interests."

"Okay, okay, I'll go get them." Drew left to get her bags from the room that she shared with her sister. She stomped down the hall, careful not to be disrespectful, but made sure that her mom knew she wasn't happy.

Plopping her bags down on the couch, Drew waited for the verdict. Her mom wasn't too happy at all when she saw how small and short some of the shirts were. Drew said, "Hold on, Mom. Before you say no, let me try them on."

Skeptically, Mrs. Daniels agreed to reserve her judgment until she had a chance to see the items on Drew.

After Drew had the first outfit on, Mrs. Daniels realized that they were layering pieces and that the shorter items were worn on top to reveal the layers beneath. "Well, now, that's not so bad. But, Drew, you have to promise me that I'm not going to catch you wearing those clothes alone or in any way that shows your belly."

"I already know that, Mom."

Mrs. Daniels raised her eyebrows, waiting.

"Okay, I promise, Mom. Really."

"Well, then, everything is fine; and I

especially like the belt you bought. It's definitely a unique piece."

Dani had been sitting quietly on the other side of the room, watching the process and waiting for the verdict. She quietly got up and went to her room, softly closed the door, and got ready for bed. She wasn't too happy, but she didn't really know what it was that was bugging her.

"Too many changes," she whispered as she drifted off to sleep.

Chapter 2

MAKING A MARK

They woke to the sound of steady rain on their windows. Because of the weather, the girls decided to ride the bus to school that day even though they much preferred to walk. Nervously, they waited on the porch and watched the corner at the end of their street for the first sign of the big yellow bus as it turned onto their street.

The bus slowed to a stop in front of their house while Dani and Drew scrambled to gather up their backpacks and purses from their perch on the front porch. Squeezing between the familiar seats, the girls stepped over the legs that spread far into the aisle and the backpacks carelessly strewn across the seat backs as they searched for an open seat to share. They headed toward the back of the bus but stopped short of the last few rows, knowing that those were reserved for the seniors. Ninth graders had to sit somewhere in the middle of the bus, and if they attempted to sit somewhere else, the seniors would make sure they paid for it. They chose a seat and settled in for the short ride.

As the bus pulled away from their house, Drew pulled out a small bag and unzipped it. Dani looked on with interest. "What's in the bag?"

Drew grinned wickedly and pulled out a tube of lipstick and waved it in Dani's face. "Look what I've got."

Drew had managed to smuggle a full set of makeup and a mirror out of the house without being seen. Dani hesitated and just watched as Drew began to apply the makeup that she hoped would make her look even older than a ninth grader.

At Drew's insistent prodding, Dani applied some sheer lip gloss and just a tiny bit of sparkly blue eye shadow to her fresh face. She liked what she saw in the mirror and handed it over to Drew, who was shaking her head.

"That's all you're going to put on?" she taunted Dani, trying to get her to use more of the makeup. "This is your chance. Are you chicken?"

Dani wouldn't take the bait—she felt guilty enough already—so Drew gave up with a shrug of her shoulders and continued to cake it on.

First, she applied some heavy black eyeliner around her eyes and then mascara to her lashes. The bumpy bus ride made the mascara difficult to apply, but eventually she managed. Then Drew took out the red lipstick and began to apply it to her full lips.

Dani gasped. "Do you have any idea what you look like?"

"I don't care," Drew replied. "I like it."

Shaking her head, Dani allowed Drew to continue; but, wanting no part of the mess, she took out a book and pretended to read while watching Drew out of the corner of her eye.

The bus slowly squealed to a stop in front of the school. The girls stood from their seats—the sticky plastic peeled from the backs of their legs leaving red, sweaty marks—and collected their things.

"Hold on," Drew said as she grabbed

Dani's sleeve. "Let's let everyone else pass, and then we'll get off." The girls waited, and when the last student passed them to get off the bus, they began to make their exit. As they stepped out into the aisle, Drew paused for a second and rolled her gray plaid knit skirt up a few inches. The skirt that had once reached Drew's knees, and the skirt that her mother was thrilled to see Drew wearing to the first day of school, became a miniskirt that Drew would never have been allowed to wear out of the house. She looked like a completely different person than the one who had kissed her mom as she left the house this morning—a person Dani wasn't sure she liked.

"What are you hoping to accomplish with this new look of yours?" Dani asked her sister, making no attempt to hide her disgust as she looked from her heavily made-up face to her now-revealed knees.

"What do I hope to accomplish? Well, sis, I intend to have a boyfriend this year; and I want to be noticed for me, not just for being one of a pair. It's time to make my mark on this school. It's time to shine," Drew replied triumphantly.

"Well, don't bump into anyone—or with all of that makeup on your face, you'll make your mark all over their shirt," Dani replied sarcastically.

"Don't be jealous, sweet sis," Drew taunted her. "You, too, can have all of this and more." Drew made an exaggerated flourish as she moved toward the front of the bus, making light of her sister's concerns as she stopped to look in the driver's rearview mirror long enough to fluff her new haircut and check her teeth for any lipstick smears. Satisfied, she smiled at her reflection, while Dani just rolled her eyes.

Exiting the bus, the girls entered the throng of students making their way toward the front door of the school. Smiling, Drew sneaked up on several of their friends. When they turned to see who was behind them, they all registered shock at Drew's appearance.

"Oh my goodness! You sure changed a lot over the summer. I really love your hair," Cara shouted above the noisy crowd.

"You look like a different person," Stacey said in shock.

"Did your mom let you dress like that?" Cara wondered.

"You two don't look anything alike any-more. I'll have no problem telling you apart now."

Dani was stopped short by this last comment. Suddenly she wasn't feeling so well and just wanted to escape the crowd. Mumbling something about making it to her homeroom class on time, she darted away, getting lost in the crowd before her sister even noticed that she was gone.

But Drew was too enthralled with the attention she was getting to pay much notice. Before entering the school, Drew pulled out her pocket mirror and reapplied her lipstick, as her fresh-faced friends looked on in awe.

Crash! While Drew was looking in the mirror, something crashed hard into her back and sent her sprawling in the grass. Dazed, she sat there for a moment trying to compose herself and then looked around to see if she could find her backpack and purse that went flying. Her mirror lay broken on the sidewalk, and her lipstick was rolling away, headed under the bus.

"Oh, man, I am so sorry."

Drew looked up to see the cutest boy in school standing over her head, offering her a hand to help her up. As she allowed herself to be righted, she looked at the boy. It was Trevor Jaymes, the captain of the varsity football team and star quarterback, in his clean, game-day uniform. Once he had her standing upright, he took off to find her things. Drew and her friends just watched as he picked up the pieces of her mirror and ran off to catch the still rolling lipstick.

Drew couldn't help but giggle when Trevor was walking toward her, trying to figure out how to twist the lipstick back down so he could put the lid on it. He pushed on it for a minute and quickly realized that wouldn't work. He looked perplexed when he saw the red smudges on his fingers. Looking for somewhere to wipe his hands, he shrugged and wiped them on his white football pants, which caused pink streaks. As she watched Trevor struggle with the lipstick, Drew couldn't contain herself any longer, so she began to laugh. Then, Trevor, determined to get that lipstick to close, pressed hard on the lid and then realized that he completely smashed the top of the stick.

"I am so sorry for everything," Trevor said as he walked toward her, appearing to blush with each step. "I think I wrecked your stuff." With a red face, he held out the broken pieces of Drew's mirror and her ruined tube of lipstick.

Drew couldn't help but laugh at his discomfort. "It's no big deal," she assured him. "It's really nothing." She noticed that he was giving her a funny look and standing there a little longer than he needed to. Drew thought he was so cute—the cutest boy in school, really. She was sure that he would never be interested in a freshman like her. He was a junior, after all. She was lucky he even stopped to talk to her.

"What's your name anyway?" Trevor asked her as he was backing away from the group.

"It's Drew," she answered him, coyly not offering any further information.

"I'm Trevor Jaymes," he shot back as he got farther away.

"Oh, I know who you are," Drew answered and then began to blush as she realized that she shouldn't have said that; she should have played it a little cooler. In order to redeem herself, she turned away before he did and flipped her long, dark hair back over her shoulders as she started to walk away, making sure her waves bounced as she walked.

"Catch you later, Drew," he called after her. Proud of herself, Drew pretended not to hear him and continued to walk away.

"Why didn't you answer him? He clearly liked you." Stacey was appalled that Drew had been rude to Trevor.

"Oh, Stacey, you have a lot to learn about boys." Drew laughed. "You never want to be too eager, and you always want to keep them guessing. They will never want what comes easily. If you play hard-to-get, it will make you look more important."

"How did you get so smart? You've never even had a boyfriend," Cara pointed out.

"While Dani was reading the actual Bible, I read *Seventeen* magazine all summer. It's the bible of boys and fashion. You girls should check it out." She pointedly looked them up and down and then laughed, teasing them. They giggled and agreed with her.

On her way to class, Drew stopped in the hallway to check out the notice board. Her friends paused with her, curious to see what she was looking for. Nodding her head, Drew turned away from the wall, looking satisfied at her find.

"What?" Cara asked. "You're so full of mystery these days. What did you see there that you liked?"

"I think I'm going to try out for the cheerleading squad, and I wanted to find out when tryouts are. That's all," Drew answered.

"Oh, I think you should," Stacey encouraged. "What does Dani think?"

"Well, that's the thing. I'd like her to do it, too. But it hardly seems to be her thing, you know?"

"Speak of the. . .well. . .angel, here she is," Cara said as Dani turned the corner and joined the group.

"Who's the angel?" Dani laughed.

"So, you and Drew are going to go out for the cheerleading squad, I hear." Stacey baited her. Drew shot daggers at Stacey with a glare that even Dani didn't miss.

"I told them you hadn't decided yet," Drew tried to assure her.

"Hadn't decided *yet*? The words 'cheerleading squad' have never even been spoken to me. I had no idea this was something I was supposed to be deciding."

"I was just thinking that it would be something fun for us to do together." Their friends slowly backed away and headed off in different directions, sure there would be an argument.

"No, you're more interested in things that you can do alone these days. It doesn't matter anyway; I am not trying out for cheerleading, and you already know that." Dani was emphatic in her answer—it was not something she wanted to do then, or ever.

"Come on, sis, you might enjoy it." Drew gave a halfhearted attempt at coaxing Dani, but she secretly hoped to be able to do it alone. "I'm not trying to find things to do that you aren't interested in. . .I'm just trying to explore other options, you know, spread my wings a bit."

"Well, I suppose you have the right to do things, just as I have the right not to do things." Dani sighed, resigned to the fact that she and her sister were pulling apart. It was inevitable, she supposed.

The bell rang, and it was time to go to class. Not wanting to end the conversation on a sad note, Drew gave her sister a hug and promised that everything would be fine. "Oh, you know me, Dan; it's probably just a phase I'm going through. Just let me try some things out and test the waters a little bit. I'll probably realize that I liked it better the other way."

"Yep, knowing you, that's true." Both girls laughed and headed off to their classes.

Chapter 3

GIVE ME A "YES!"

"Girls, I need you all to line up. We're going to teach you a cheer and then have you perform it. What we are looking for is style, smile, and choreography." The cheerleading coach, Tracy, was leading the after-school tryouts out on the football field on Friday afternoon. "If you get tapped on the shoulder, it means that we're asking you to step out of the tryouts. Please understand that we appreciate your efforts, but there are only seven freshman positions available for the junior varsity squad and about thirty girls who are trying out for them. At this time, though, I'm going to turn things over to our head cheerleader, Kallie, who will teach you the routine. Good luck, girls."

The coach sat on a chair on the sidelines with a clipboard poised on her lap for note-taking. The thirty hopefuls who were trying out for the squad lined up on the field awaiting their instructions. Drew looked up and down the two rows of girls, sizing up her competition. She knew at least two of the girls had prior dance experience and three others had been in gymnastics with Drew. She wasn't sure about the dancers, but she knew that she was more skilled than the other gymnasts. She also noticed that there were many girls who weren't really contenders for a spot for various other reasons. As she waited, she began to grow a bit more confident that she could secure one of the spots on the team.

Kallie took her position in front of the girls, and two of her cheerleaders joined her and flanked her, one on each side. She began to teach the girls the cheer that they would have to learn for their audition. First, Kallie and the other two cheerleaders performed the cheer three times for the girls to watch. One thing that Drew took note of was that they smiled the entire time, even while they were shouting the cheer. After they had the chance to watch it three times, Kallie took them through the moves and the words one section at a time. It was unnerving to see that Tracy, the coach, had begun to move about the rows of girls, looking at them closely as they practiced. A few times, she tapped girls on the shoulder to let them know that they were excused from the tryouts. That just made Drew work even harder at keeping that smile on her face and getting the moves just right.

After almost two hours of practicing, they were almost ready to perform the cheer as their final audition for Coach Tracy, who had left the field about an hour earlier. Before she went off to find the coach, Kallie asked, "Is there anyone who can do a back flip and would feel comfortable performing it for your audition? Since you have all done so well, I have a little surprise in mind for Tracy."

Three girls raised their hands, including Drew. Kallie gave each of them a chance to show her their back flip so she could select one girl to perform it for Tracy in the audition. First was Delaney. She was a decent gymnast and, if she nailed it, she could possibly be the best one to perform the flip, but she was often inconsistent, as Drew knew from gymnastics practice and meets. So Drew was anxious to see how she did.

Delaney stood back and set off on a little run, did a round-off, and then a back flip. Her moves were fine, but she stumbled at the end rather than standing tall and solid. Her stumble caused her to lose her concentration, so her smile wavered.

Drew didn't know the second girl but was glad to see that her back flip was nowhere near as good as Delaney's was. It was Drew's turn. She wanted to nail this so badly. She looked down the line of girls who were waiting to see how she'd perform. She put a big smile on her face and set off on her run, preparing for her flip. She, too, did a round-off first and then a flip. It was perfect! She ended without a wobble and raised her arms as high as she could with a big smile on her face the entire time.

Kallie announced that Drew would be performing the trick at the end of their audition. They ran through the cheer one more time, adding in the specialty move that would be a surprise to Tracy.

After seeing the finished product, before she called Tracy back to view the final audition, Kallie told the girls her thoughts. "I am so surprised and impressed with this freshman group. You have done a fantastic job, and it's going to be a very difficult choice for us to make. I wish you all the best of luck." With that, she went to find Tracy, leaving the girls to take a break while she was gone.

"Okay, girls, let's see what you've got." Tracy came back, eager to see what the girls had learned and more than ready to begin the selection process for the new junior varsity cheerleading squad.

"Ready? Begin," Kallie shouted, calling for the cheer to start. The girls waited the two seconds they were supposed to and then began. The cheer went remarkably well except for a few girls who forgot the words and a few others who missed their cues. They were tapped on the shoulders and asked to step out of line—they were out of the running. At the end of the cheer, Drew poised herself to perform her big finish. It went perfectly, even better than the first time. She was exhilarated and proud when the cheer was over and they all turned to look at Tracy.

"I must say, girls, I am very impressed. You went above and beyond what was called for and even added difficulty to the routine. This is going to be a difficult selection process. You can look at the bulletin board outside of the sports office for the results on Monday morning."

Drew left the tryouts excited and hopeful, but as she walked home, she became worried. It was sure to be a long weekend while Drew anxiously awaited the results of her cheerleading tryouts.

"Of course you'll make the squad. You got to do the big finish that impressed the coach," Dani tried to assure her numerous times. Drew even showed Dani the cheer to get her opinion. "You look like a natural-born cheerleader, Drew. Stop worrying about it." Dani was so irritated by the end of the weekend that she couldn't wait to get the results on Monday morning either, just so the constant talking about it would be over.

Monday morning couldn't have come soon enough for Drew. She jumped out of bed as soon as the alarm began to ring instead of pushing the SNOOZE button three times like she usually did. She yanked on the window shades, which opened with a loud *snap* and flapped as they rolled up. Bright sunlight streamed through the windows and filled the pretty, pink room. Dani began to stir and then groaned as she tried to open her eyes to the bright light.

"What are you doing?" Dani whined, rubbing her eyes. "We have more time to sleep. Why are you torturing me?"

"Dani! You need to get up right away. We have to leave for school as soon as we can get ready." Drew was so excited, she could barely contain it.

"Is this because of the cheerleading list?" Dani asked with obvious irritation.

"Of course. I've been waiting all weekend to see the results. Now come on." Drew pulled on the floral quilt that Dani held up by her chin.

"Okay, okay, I'm getting up. Give me a second."

"I'm going to use the bathroom. Please, please, please don't go back to sleep," Drew begged.

After Drew prodded Dani through breakfast and hurried her into dressing and packing her backpack, they loaded in the car and waited for their mom. Mrs. Daniels had agreed to drive them so Drew wouldn't have to wait for the bus or walk. "Come on, Mom," Drew called through the open window.

"I'm coming; hold your horses," Mrs. Daniels laughingly said as she got into the car.

As soon as they got to school, Drew said a hurried good-bye to her mom and Dani and then jumped out of the car and sprinted toward the building. Dani quietly watched her go, shaking her head with a smile and wondering how they could be identical twins, yet so incredibly different.

Drew ran right to the sports office and stared at the bulletin board, so anxious to see the list of the new squad members but afraid at the same time that she hadn't made it. Going down the list of names. . ."Stephanie Akers, Melanie Coldwell, Emily Frankle. . ." A lump caught in Drew's throat as she realized that the alphabetical list of the names of the girls who had been selected to be a part of the JV squad, the varsity squad, and the dance team didn't include her name. She hadn't made the team.

Not knowing what to think and not wanting to face anyone for fear of bursting into tears, Drew just stood there staring at the list. She was so disappointed and, admittedly, surprised. Continuing down the list, she read the names and sighed as she neared the bottom.

Still having trouble dealing with the news, she decided to read the list again. Starting at the top, she made her way to the bottom. Her name never magically appeared among the other girls' names. As she was about to give up and step away, she stopped short as she noticed her name at the bottom of the page, separate from the list. She stepped a little closer and read the note in italics: *"Drew Daniels; Junior Varsity Cheerleading Squad Captain."*

So she had made the team! With a huge sigh of relief, Drew realized that not only had she made the team, but she was given the high honor of being the team captain. Her heart was beating wildly in her excitement.

"Drew, welcome to the team." Coach Tracy walked up behind her and patted her on the back.

"Thank you so much, Coach. I didn't see my name at first, and I panicked a little. I wanted this so badly, and I appreciate the extra responsibility you've given me by making me team captain. I didn't even know that was a possibility for a freshman."

"Well, Drew, your tryouts were exceptional; you definitely stood out among your peers, and you went above and beyond what the rest of the girls did. I also spoke with a few of your teachers from last year. It seems that you have a reputation for being a kind and fair leader in school. So it was a logical choice. I'm sure you'll do very well."

"Thanks for the vote of confidence, Coach," Drew said. "I promise I won't let you down."

It was an exciting day for Drew. Her new position on the cheerleading squad and her role as captain gave her instant celebrity among the freshman class.

Dani, on the other hand, plodded through her day with growing resentment of Drew's new focus and popularity. She didn't want to be jealous, and it wasn't exactly jealousy that she felt. She just felt left out. Dani and Drew had been inseparable, a single unit, for their whole lives up until this first week of school. All of a sudden everything changed and she was left standing alone, and Drew didn't even seem to notice. It seemed like Drew wanted to be as far from her as possible and didn't even seem to miss her and the tight bond they had, while Dani felt like a part of her had died.

Everywhere she went that day, people were saying things like, "Drew is the captain of the cheerleaders—isn't that fabulous? She's going to look so cute in the uniform." Or, "Why didn't you try out for the squad, Dani? I'm sure you'd have made it like Drew did." Or, "What are you going to do with all of your time now that Drew will be so busy with practices and games? I'll bet she'll make a lot of new friends, too." Each comment was like a knife through her heart. By the end of the day, all she wanted was to be home, in her room, alone.

Chapter 4

SQUEAKY CLEAN

Two days later, on the bus ride home, Drew was still unrelenting with her annoying chatter about her news. She wanted to talk about her schedule, her uniform, her practices, her leadership goals, her future plans—it was like this one moment, this one thing, had redefined her life.

"You know, Drew, I seriously think you need to settle down. I'm happy for you and all, but you're taking it a little too far, don't you think?" Dani finally had to ask her sister.

After looking at her for a moment, Drew asked, "What has gotten into you lately? You have been so glum this whole week and you've hardly said a word all day." After Dani remained silent for a few seconds, Drew said, "Ah, I get it. You're jealous. Don't forget, I tried to get you to try out, too."

"Drew, I'm not jealous. . .I'm. . .oh, forget it, you'll never understand if you haven't figured it out already."

At that moment, the bus pulled up in front of their house and the doors squeaked open to let them off. Once in the house, Drew wanted to finish their talk, so she started to ask Dani more questions, but Dani held up her hand to stop her. "Let's just let it go for now. I would like to salvage part of this day. We have a couple of hours until youth group tonight, so let's do something together."

"That's a good idea, but first I have to call Stephanie. She said she has some big news for me. I think Trevor asked her about me or something. When I'm done, we can do our nails or watch TV or something."

"Oh, never mind, I'll just do my homework," Dani answered, not wanting to be second choice to Drew's other, newer friends.

"Suit yourself," Drew replied cheerfully as she grabbed the phone and headed up the stairs to their bedroom. Dani settled on the couch to do her homework and watch some TV. They only had an hour until their mom was due home anyway. They would have dinner and then go to church. Tonight was supposed to be a special night at youth group, and Dani had been looking forward to it. Pastor Steve had cooked up a surprise for them, so she didn't know what would be happening. She hoped it would be really good; she needed the diversion.

The minutes ticked by, and it was ten minutes to five before Dani even realized it. Drew was still upstairs on the phone, but Dani was finished with today's homework and had gotten a start on some that wasn't due until later in the week.

Finally, Drew came back downstairs and replaced the phone in its cradle on the wall. "I wonder what Mom's planning for dinner tonight," Drew said, looking for clues in the refrigerator. At just that moment, Drew stopped in her tracks when she heard the garage door begin to open. "Oh no." She gasped. "Stall Mom. I haven't washed off my makeup yet." She ran up the stairs to the bathroom where she slammed the door.

Mrs. Daniels came in, arms laden with

grocery bags. "Girls, I could use a hand here," she called, cheerfully summoning the girls to come help her unload and put away the groceries.

"I'll help you, Mom," Dani offered, immediately getting off the couch.

"Great, where's Drew?" Mrs. Daniels asked as Dani started to unpack the plastic grocery bags.

"Last I heard she was in the bathroom. She should be right down," Drew answered, being very careful not to lie.

"How was your day, sweetie?" Mrs. Daniels asked Dani.

"Oh, it was okay, Mom. Nothing special to report from me. . ." Dani smiled and held up her hand to fend off what she knew was going to be her Mom's next question. "And don't ask; I'm sure Drew'll want to fill you in about her day herself." Dani giggled when her mom closed her mouth. It was clear that she was about to ask about Drew's day, but Dani was tired of talking about Drew. She hurriedly put away the groceries so she could excuse herself from the kitchen before Drew came down. The last thing she wanted was to have to endure yet another conversation having anything to do with cheerleading.

"I'm done, Mom. I'll be upstairs if you need me." She breezed through the doorway just as Drew, freshly scrubbed, came into the kitchen.

"Hi, Mom. Guess what?"

Dani hurried up the stairs so that she didn't have to hear what Drew was about to say.

In the kitchen, Mrs. Daniels listened to Drew recount the details of her day. Drew was bubbling over with excitement about her newfound popularity. Although Mrs. Daniels was truly happy for her daughter, she did have some concerns.

"Sweetheart, I'm so proud of you. I think it's fantastic that you made the team and even better that you were selected to be a leader. What a great honor. Like I've been saying, that sort of thing looks wonderful on college applications too. But. . ."

"I know, Mom. It's really exciting," Drew interrupted. "Nothing like this has ever happened to me. It's weird doing it without Dani, though. But it's probably for the best," Drew explained. "We can't do everything together forever."

"Well, sweetie, just be careful that you don't leave your sister behind and make her take a backseat to your new interests. She's your sister; she's your best friend. She will always be a part of your life. Other friends, teams, interests. . .they will all come and go. But Dani will be the one person who will always be by your side. Just don't leave her in your dust as you pursue this new independence that you seem to want so badly."

"I'm not being insensitive, am I, Mom? I don't want to hurt her. I'm really not trying to."

"I know you're not trying to hurt her. But sometimes people get hurt even with the best of intentions. Think back over the past week. Have you even asked her anything about her life or have you just spent the last few days talking about yourself? Show some interest in her, and let her know that you haven't completely changed and that she is still just as important to you as she was before all of these changes started."

"Oh no, Mom. . ." Drew's face fell when she remembered. "Dani asked me to do something with her this afternoon and I told her I had to call Stephanie first. I stayed on the phone until just about the time you came home." Drew left out the part about needing to scrub the makeup off her face before her mom saw her.

"That's the kind of thing I'm talking

about. By doing that, Drew, you basically told her that she wasn't as important as your new friends. I know that you don't feel that way, but you have to think about how Dani might feel. Do you understand what I mean?"

"Yeah, Mom, I get what you're saying. I'll be more careful and try to be more thoughtful."

"That's all you can do, sweetie. Now I'm going to heat up dinner. You girls get ready for church. We need to leave in about forty-five minutes, and your dad should be home in fifteen minutes. So we'll sneak dinner in before we leave."

"Sounds good." Drew took off up the stairs planning on getting changed for church but also hoping to patch things up with Dani.

Arriving at church with barely enough time to get to their groups, Mr. and Mrs. Daniels headed off to their adult Bible study class while Dani and Drew went to youth group in the building behind the church. It had once been a parsonage before the church was completely rebuilt and updated. At that time, the old house was given to the youth group and converted into an activity center. It had couches and chairs, a big screen TV for watching movies, some game tables, a foosball table and pool table, as well as a kitchen stocked with basics and cooking equipment. It was a great place to hang out.

Tonight, though, there was something special going on. The girls had been speculating on the drive over as to what it could be. Drew thought it was probably a pizza party, but Dani didn't think that was special enough to warrant all the hush-hush and surprise talk. Dani thought there was probably a special guest due to be there. But she had no idea who it could be.

With no fanfare or introduction, the doors opened and in walked three players from the Pittsburgh Steelers football team and two of their cheerleaders—all dressed in uniform. Drew was immediately enthralled and stared with her mouth open for at least a full minute. She finally got over her shock and looked at Dani in excitement.

Dani sat quietly, shaking her head, thinking her day couldn't possibly get any worse. She had definitely had enough of anything to do with cheerleading for a very long time; and she certainly never expected to have to face it at church, too. But it looked like she was going to have to deal with it for at least another couple of hours.

One of the players went to the front of the group and introduced himself for those who didn't know who he was. "Hi, everyone. I'm Shane Sutter. I'm one of the quarterbacks from the Pittsburgh Steelers. You're all probably wondering why we're here with you today." When everyone excitedly acknowledged his introduction and nodded in agreement, Shane continued. "Well, the five of us have a special calling or a special desire, you might say, to work with teens. We have all had very different experiences, but the one thing that we share in common is that our different roads have led us to a point where we realized that we could do nothing without Jesus. Tonight we'd each like to share a little bit about our pasts and how we came to know Jesus, and then we'll give you guys a chance to ask us questions. We're pretty informal so just relax, grab a drink or a snack, and let's get started."

No one moved to get a snack. They were all too excited to hear what their celebrities had to say. One by one, the athletes shared their testimonies with the teens. A common thread through the stories was the poor decisions that they made that led to rough patches in their lives. Shane told the story of a time when he was playing football in college and he got the surprise of his life when his girlfriend got pregnant. He recounted the fears and doubts of sticking by her side through the pregnancy and then the agonizing reality of giving the baby up for adoption.

"One thing I learned through that whole experience, something I still carry with me today, is that my choices are never just about me. Other lives are affected by what I do. I have to be willing to live with seeing the people I love hurt by my mistakes, or I need to make a different choice. The girl I was dating during all of that, well, her life was turned upside down. She was in her first year of college, and she was basically alone and had to go through a pregnancy, a birth, and then she had to let go of that baby. She will never, ever be the same. Also, think about that baby. That baby is a human being and deserved two loving parents. We believe that she got that, but the heartache of knowing she was given up for adoption will affect her one day. Our parents were also gravely affected. They had to grieve the loss of a grandchild they would never know.

"I had believed," Shane continued, "that my choices were just that—mine. I felt that people should stay out of my life and let me make my decisions and my mistakes if I wanted to. But I couldn't have been more wrong. My personal and most private decisions affected everyone I cared about. The hardest part of facing my consequences was watching the people I loved suffer. And there was nothing I could do about it; it was too late."

Finishing up his testimony, Shane turned it over to Jodie, one of the cheerleaders. She shared a much different experience. "I was in high school, a junior at the time, and I wanted to date a boy who was a junior in college. My parents forbade me to see him because he was too old and there was something about him they just didn't like, but they couldn't quite identify what it was. I thought that they were just being judgmental and were wrong, so I sneaked around and dated him anyway. To make a very long story short, one night he slipped something into my cola; and when I became affected by the drug, he raped me.

"My parents had been right; but, because they couldn't convince me, I ignored them. In retrospect I wonder just who I thought I was. I mean, what arrogance I must have had to think that I knew more than them. If only I had just heeded their warning and obeyed their wishes, I would have avoided a lifetime of pain. I suffered tremendous loss, years of anguish, and it took years of counseling before I felt somewhat whole again. It wasn't until I found the Lord that I really began to love myself again and feel restored to a level of innocence that had been stripped from me.

"The main thing that I'd like for you to take from my story is that you are all just like me. You think you know so much and that your parents are old-fashioned, right? Don't buy into that lie from the enemy. He wants you to believe that you know better, because when you question your parents and doubt their word and are willing to disobey them, that's when he can sneak in and get control of your life. Who do you want to be in control of your life? Choose God, and then let Him work through your parents to lead you down the right road."

They continued on with the testimonies, and when they had about thirty minutes left in the evening, Shane stood up again and said, "We're going to try something a little different. We'd like to separate into two groups. The boys will come with me and the other players outside, and the girls will stay here with Jodie and Becky. We thought that it might give you all a little more freedom to talk about the things that really matter most to you and also to give us the opportunity to address issues that pertain to girls and boys separately. How does that sound?"

With a chorus of agreement, the students began to shuffle positions—the boys went outside and the girls arranged their seating so that they were a little more comfortable and their circle a little tighter.

Jodie started off the question-and-answer time by saying, "Do any of you have a topic or a question that you'd like to ask us?"

Dani raised her hand. "I have a question. It's really a two-parter, if that's okay." When they nodded and said it was fine, she continued. "Were you both on the cheerleading squad and really popular in high school? And if so, do you think the popularity influenced you in making poor decisions?"

"Great question. Do you want to answer that, Becky?"

"Yeah, for me it was definitely a factor. I loved my position on the squad, and it did help me become very popular in school. In that role, I made some bad choices so that I would look cool and keep my 'popular status.' I was a leader in both the good things and in the bad things."

"Same for me," Jodie said. "I wanted to be popular, and cheerleading helped me get there; but it took a lot of dumb decisions and mistakes to keep me there. I just wish I had known that the people who wanted me to behave that way weren't really my friends. If I had really understood that, it may have made it easier to say no to some things."

"How about some other questions?"

"I have one." A new girl named Megan raised her hand. "My boyfriend has been pressuring me to go further with him physically than I feel comfortable going. What do you think I should do?"

"Honestly," Jodie said, "I think you should find a new boyfriend. If you are with someone who is pressuring you to do anything at all, then he doesn't really, truly care about you. He's only interested in how you can benefit him. If he really cared about you, he would care about what you're ready for or not ready for. Plus, if you have a spiritual foundation and you're trying to follow God's will, wouldn't you want someone who supported that and wanted the same thing?"

"But," Megan asked, "aren't all boys like that? I mean, are there any who wouldn't put the pressure on?"

"Of course there are. There are boys here in this meeting tonight who are worried about protecting their own purity. Those are the kinds of boys you want to be with."

"So, maybe where I meet them is part of the problem?" Megan was looking for clarification, and all of the other girls were hanging on Jodie's words.

"Well, you can meet a good boy at school and a bad seed at church. The location isn't a guarantee, but it sure is a good start. But girls, let's consider something else entirely. What if you didn't have a boyfriend at all right now? You know, God has a perfect plan for your life. He set aside this period of growing up to be the time when He shapes you into the confident, secure, and godly woman that He wants you to be. That process is so much more difficult if you're already trying to act like an adult and have adult relationships. I mean, do you really think that you will meet and date a boy now who will become your husband later? If you don't think so, then what's the point of dating now? You're only opening yourself up for hardship and pain." Jodie paused and looked around the group, making eye contact with as many girls as possible.

"If I sound opinionated on this subject, it's because I am. I only wish someone could have gotten through to me when I was your age. I wish I had spent less time acting like a grown-up and more time actually growing up. I let my identity be shaped by whether or not boys liked me. I forgot that I am perfect and beautiful in God's eyes already. Don't make the same mistake I did, okay?"

They continued talking until it was time to go home. When it was over, Drew and Dani picked up their purses and started to head for the door. "Hang on a second, Dani. I want to talk to Jodie privately." Drew ran over to Jodie and told her that she was fantastic.

Jodie said, "You have that look in your eye, Drew. The same look I had when I was your age. I just hope you remember some of the things we said tonight. Here, take my e-mail address. If you ever find that you're in need of someone to talk to, shoot me a note. Okay?"

"Thanks so much. I really appreciate you guys coming here and doing this. It was awesome." They briefly hugged, and then Drew was on her way to find her family. She was much more excited about having had the chance to meet real cheerleaders than she was about anything they had said. She put Jodie's e-mail address in her wallet in a safe place just in case she needed it sometime.

Chapter 5

IS IT A DATE?

The bleachers were full and the crowd roared. It was the first home game of the season. Students, family members, and locals had all turned out wearing their Panthers shirts and hats, and waved their flags in support of the football team. The vendors made their way through the throng of people, selling their hot dogs and popcorn. Young kids played under and behind the bleachers. Dani and her parents got there early enough to find seats in the fourth row of the bleachers and were all eager to support Drew at her first game.

Dani couldn't help herself; she got into the excitement of the event and the energy that the crowd was creating. She sat forward in her seat and tried to find Drew among the cheerleaders on the sidelines. They huddled in a circle, getting a pep talk from the captain. . .oh, wait. It was Drew giving the pep talk; she *was* the captain. All of a sudden, feelings of jealousy and resentment started to fade away as Dani became proud of her sister. She watched her sister lead the squad; Drew was right where she was supposed to be. Dani vowed to herself that, from then on, she would support Drew and encourage her.

The cheerleaders all let out a little yell for team spirit and then broke to begin their opening cheer. The junior varsity squad customarily opened with a cheer-and-dance routine to set the tone for the game. Then they spent their time during the game on the sidelines cheering for their team and leading the crowd. So, at five minutes before kick-off, they took off their sweatshirts and bounded out onto the field into their formation.

"Ready! Begin!" Drew shouted off the cue to start the routine. Music started and the girls began their dance. They were perfectly in sync and looked fantastic on the field in their red and gold skirts that floated around their thighs, and their sleeveless white shirts with the yellow and black chevron that said PANTHERS in the middle. Even Dani had to admit that they really looked cool. In the middle of the routine, there was a pause in the music and the girls began a cheer for their team. It was exciting and stirred up the crowd's energy even more. The music began just as the cheer ended, and they finished up their dance routine with a pyramid. In front of the pyramid, Drew ran and did a round-off and two back flips to finish up the routine with a flourish.

The crowd was worked into a frenzy. The JV cheerleaders had been exciting to watch, a more talented group than any JV team before them. It set the tone for the whole event. "I can't believe how great those girls were," Mrs. Daniels leaned over and said to her husband and Dani.

"I know, Mom. Drew really looks like she was meant to be doing that, doesn't she?"

"I've never been so proud of her," Mr. Daniels said. "Looks like all of those years of dance and gymnastics have paid off. And it's not just that, she's a real leader. Those girls look up to her."

"I'm really happy for Drew, and I feel bad for being so upset about it all. But I do hope that I can find my niche somehow," Dani admitted.

"You will, sweetie," Mrs. Daniels promised. "You'll figure out what excites you and gives you the same joy that Drew has found. It might be a sport, a club, or maybe something academic like debate team or the class play."

"Oh, I like the sound of debate team, Mom. I might have to look into that."

"Dani, that's a great idea," Mr. Daniels encouraged. "If you're serious about becoming a lawyer one day, debate team would be a great experience for you."

Dani sat back, deep in thought as she contemplated the possibilities and recognized that being different from her sister might not be as horrible as she had once thought.

While they were on the bleachers, waiting for the cheerleaders to come out at halftime, Drew was on the sidelines cheering for the team. Every once in a while, she took a break to get a drink of water from the team cooler. Whenever she went for a drink, her family couldn't see her inside the team shelter. So they also couldn't see the boy she was talking to every chance she got.

Whenever she saw that he wasn't playing on the field, she went to get a drink of water; and each time, he was standing right there by the cooler—Trevor Jaymes. The sight of him made Drew get a little jittery, but she knew she had to play it cool. She confidently walked right up to the cooler and drew some water out into a cup that was provided.

"Hi, boys." Without looking directly at Trevor, she tossed her hair over her shoulders and left the shelter to join her team. Out of the corner of her eye, she could tell that they were watching her; and it seemed that they were talking about her, too. She was very careful not to let them know that she was paying attention to them.

A little while later, before the halftime show, Drew went back for another drink of water. She timed it perfectly so that she would already be there when Trevor got pulled from the game for a rest. He'd had a perfect game so far; but he would wear out if he didn't get a break, and the team needed him fresh to finish up the game later. He came into the team shelter to get a drink of water just as Drew finished filling up her cup.

"Well, hello again, Drew," Trevor said, making sure to use her name so she would know he hadn't forgotten it.

"Hi, Trevor. Great game," Drew said

enthusiastically. It was time to let her guard down a little so that, if he were interested in her, he would know there was a chance at gaining her attention.

"Thanks a lot," he replied with surprise. "I didn't think you cheerleaders even watched the game."

"Ha, funny. Of course we do. How else would we know when to cheer?"

"Well, you might, but I guarantee you that half of your team just waits for your cue and follows suit. But at least you're watching me. . . er. . .I mean us."

"Oh, I'm watching, all right," Drew replied flirtatiously as she walked back to her squad.

"Hey, Steph, what's the score?" she asked her teammate as a test to see if she was watching.

"Um, well, a minute ago it was, um. . .I'm not sure." Stephanie had no idea what the score was.

Hmm, Drew thought, surprised that Stephanie hadn't been paying attention, since the coach had just stressed the importance of that at their last practice. *I'm going to have to keep an eye on that and maybe even bring it up again in practice.* They were there to support the team, and it was much more credible if they actually knew why they were cheering.

The game continued on, and Drew had a blast. Her family did, too, and they watched her throughout the entire game. She was definitely in her element. The halftime show was perfect. It was mainly the varsity cheerleaders, but the JV squad also had several parts in the routine which turned it into a great big field show.

Drew was exhausted when the game was over and was about ready to head to the car to meet her family after she had packed up her things. She suddenly felt a presence behind her and turned to see Trevor watching her, waiting to be noticed.

"Hey. What's up?" Drew asked casually.

"Well, Miss Daniels, I was wondering if you'd like to grab a bite to eat. A bunch of us are going to The Grill. I can have you home in about an hour, give or take a few considering the crowds," he promised, realizing that it was already pretty late.

"I'd love to. Let me go tell my parents and sister that I'll be home soon." Drew didn't tell him that she would have to beg and perhaps even tell a little white lie to get permission. But there was no way she wasn't going to go. She ran quickly over to her family who were waiting for her at the car.

"Sweetie, you were awesome." Mrs. Daniels pulled her into a tight hug.

"I agree, Drew," Mr. Daniels chimed in. "You were definitely in your element. I've never been more proud of you."

"Me, too, sis. I'm sorry I've given you a hard time about it all. You're clearly doing what you are supposed to be doing," Dani admitted.

Drew was thrilled to hear their comments but didn't want to keep Trevor waiting. She hated that she'd have to lie. . .but it wasn't really a total lie. . .she hoped.

"Thanks, everyone. Mom, Dad, I'd like to go with the team and get a bite to eat. It's kind of customary, and being the captain, I should probably be there. We're going to The Grill, and I'd be home in about an hour depending on how busy it is. Is that okay?"

"Sure, sweetie. An adult will give you a ride home? If not, be sure to call for a ride. Okay?" When Drew promised that she would, her mom asked, "Hey, can Dani go?"

"No way, Mom," Dani jumped in, much

to Drew's relief. "This isn't my thing. I'm not tagging along. I don't even want to go anyway. I'm too tired."

Drew hugged everyone and then went back to find the group. To her surprise, everyone was gone except for Trevor. "You ready? They're saving seats for us."

"Yep, all set. Let me grab my bags, and we can go."

The Grill was bustling with excitement as the football team and cheerleaders filled the rich mahogany booths. They were all starving after the big game and were excited over their win. Spirits were high, and the noise level was deafening. Drew and Trevor navigated through the high fives and congratulatory claps on the back as Trevor's teammates congratulated him on the win. His big, toothy grin revealed just how much he reveled in the recognition.

The crowd pressed in so tightly that it was difficult for the two to squeeze through, and Trevor kept losing Drew as people swarmed around him. Finally, he just grabbed her hand and held on until they finally made their way to their seats. "Phew," Trevor said as they slid into the booth. "We made it."

"Yep, it was looking kind of iffy there for a minute." Drew laughed.

"Hey, Drew, I haven't had a chance to tell you this yet." Trevor leaned over the table and said privately, "You did a really great job tonight."

"Oh yeah," Buck said, overhearing Trevor's words.

"You really did do a great job. I've never seen the JV squad look so awesome," Buck's girlfriend, Sam, added.

"Trevor said you were cute the day he bumped into you accidentally, *wink, wink,* but I had no idea that he was talking about the captain of the cheerleaders." Buck revealed a little more about Trevor's little accident than Trevor would have liked, judging by his reddened face.

"I didn't know she was even going out for cheerleading that day. I thought she was just a cute freshman."

"That's enough about me." Drew laughed, her face reddening. "This is getting awkward; I'm right here."

"Okay, fair enough. We'll talk about you later then," Buck teased.

"Don't let him get to you. He only picks on people he likes," Sam informed Drew.

"Oh, I think I can hold my own." Drew laughed again. "But I'm starving. I wonder if we even have time to order, though. I have to be home in about an hour."

"Food's on its way. We already ordered." Buck was proud to surprise them.

"Good move, dude. This crowd is crazy."

At that moment, the waitress appeared at their table and set down Cokes for Trevor and Drew and cheeseburgers and fries all around. They dug in with a vengeance, and all conversation stopped. A cheeseburger had never tasted so good.

After they had eaten, it was time for Trevor to get Drew home. On the way to the car he said, "We'd better get you home so that your parents trust me for the next time we go out."

"Oh?" Drew coyly asked. "What makes you so sure there's going to be a next time?"

"Well, I mean, only if you want to. . ." Trevor stammered.

"Oh, well, in *that* case," Drew teased, "I'm sure there will be many next times."

Trevor visibly relaxed when he heard that and, without thinking, reached over and took her hand. Drew had never had her hand held by a boy she liked—and she enjoyed the little tingle of excitement it gave her. She giggled just as they reached the car. Trevor tucked her into her seat and shut her door, then went around to the other side. Before he got in, Drew wiped the dampness off her hand and placed it on the console between the two seats—just in case he'd like to hold it again.

He held her hand in silence—they were both taking in the moment and were lost in thought, so they forgot to speak out loud—the whole way to her house. As they pulled into her driveway, Drew turned to Trevor and thanked him for a great time. He promised to call her but would also see her in school Monday.

Drew hurriedly got out of the car so that her parents wouldn't come to the door and see that she was alone in the car with a boy. She ran into the house excitedly and started talking the moment she got into the living room where her parents were. She began filling them in with all sorts of needless details about who was there, what they ate, how busy it was, how fun it was to be a part of the team. . .so they wouldn't think to question her about who drove her home. They were tired, so it worked. Drew excused herself to head upstairs to bed, and Dani, who had been sitting on the couch, followed her up.

"I saw you pull in the driveway. You're going to need to be more careful, sis," Dani warned. "You're making some important choices, and you've never been one to lie to Mom and Dad or disobey so blatantly."

"I didn't lie. . .they didn't even ask how I got home."

"Not telling the truth is the same as lying. And you did break one of their rules—several, actually. You led them to believe that you were trustworthy, and they gave you that trust. Just think hard next time about whether or not it's really worth it to lose that trust or even damage it a little. I just don't want to see you get hurt."

Dani heard her softly snoring. "Drew. . . Drew. . .you there?"

But Drew had fallen asleep already. Chuckling to herself, Dani rolled over and said a little prayer for her sister before nodding off herself.

Chapter 6

GOD'S WAY?

The girls awoke to the smell of bacon, as they normally did every Sunday morning before church. Drew and Dani were both very tired after a long weekend that started with game night on Friday and continued with family activities on Saturday. They pulled their matching comforters up over their heads and attempted to bury themselves under the covers to get a few more minutes of sleep. Their mom knocked softly on the door before she opened it. She peered in and saw the girls were still in their beds. Coming into the room, she opened the window shades to let in some light, and the girls groaned when the brightness hit their eyes.

"Mom, we need just a few more minutes, ple–e–e–ease?" Drew begged.

"Now girls, it's time to get ready for church. Don't make me lower your curfew—I'll do that if church becomes affected by your staying up too late on the weekends."

"All right, all right, I'm getting up." Drew put an effort forth by sitting up in her bed. Dani already had her feet on the floor and was sitting on the side of her bed. "We'll be down in a few minutes, Mom."

"Now, girls, don't lie back down," Mrs. Daniels warned them as she left the room. It took all of Drew's effort, amid a lot of sleepy moaning and eye rubbing, to continue getting up when all she wanted to do was to crawl back under the covers.

Slowly, both girls got out of their beds and headed for the bathroom they shared. Silently, Dani brushed her teeth and washed her face while Drew got her things together for a shower.

"We really need to wake up," Drew said.

"Yeah, we sure do. I can't believe how tired I am," Dani admitted.

"Yesterday was a big day. But we better get

it together, or Mom and Dad aren't going to be happy. We have to show them that we can handle being up late and not struggle in the morning. It will help our cause for staying out later and going on dates."

"Um, *our* cause?" Dani laughed. "That's *your* cause right now, sis. Not me. I have nothing to do with it."

"Oh, believe me, your day will come; and you'll be so glad that I paved the way by getting them on our side now."

"Whatever you say." Dani laughed again, shaking her head. "Mom and Dad aren't going to just let you start dating and staying out late, you know. When are you going to tell them about Trevor, anyway?"

"When there's something to tell, I guess." Drew looked annoyed.

"Oh, I'm pretty sure Mom and Dad would feel that line had been crossed already." She put up her hand to keep Drew from defending herself any further. "I just hope you know what you're doing. I care about what happens to you, and I don't want to see you get hurt."

Drew looked at the reflection staring back at her from the mirror—sometimes she forgot whether she was looking at herself or her sister. To whichever one it was, or maybe to both of them, she confidently said, "I have everything under control."

Drew jumped in to take a quick shower to help wake her up. Dani continued getting ready in silence. The silence started to get to Drew, though. So she decided that it was up to her to break the ice and get her sister cheered up. She unhooked the shower massage head and turned the water from hot to very cold. She quietly reached forward and pulled back the curtain.

Being careful not to get Dani's hair wet, because that would just be cruel, she aimed the wet, pulsating stream at Dani's body, soaking her pajamas with icy cold water. Dani shrieked in surprise when the water hit her skin. At first she looked angry, but when she saw Drew's face all aglow with mischief, she dissolved into laughter. It was a tension breaker they both needed.

"You just wait! I'll get you back when you least expect it," Dani warned.

"I look forward to it, sis." Drew's eyes twinkled as she returned to her shower, and Dani had a big smile on her face as she toweled off before leaving the bathroom to get dressed.

" 'I have everything under control,' " the preacher began his sermon. "Do we say that to God? If we don't come right out and say it, don't we act like it sometimes? You know, we have access to God's plan all laid out for us. We have His perfect guidelines, and we *know* His will. We know which actions grieve Him, and there is seldom a question about what is right in His eyes. We get all of that information, that insight into who He is and what He wants for us and from us, right from His Word, the Bible. Yet, we often walk through life acting as though we have no clue about what to do. We say with our words and our actions that we have everything under control—basically, that we are going to ignore God's desires and plans for us because we know better. What drives that mindset? I'll tell you what it is—it's pure selfishness. It's a heart that is closed off to the will of God and is selfishly pursuing personal plans and desires while forsaking God in the process.

"Do you find yourself in a situation where

you know that what you are doing is wrong, yet you turn off the inner voice that cries out to your spirit? Do you ignore God because you are so dead set on doing whatever it is that you want to do?"

Dani and Drew sat next to each other; they looked like almost the same person. However, they had completely different postures as they listened to the preacher. Dani sat with her head down, thinking. She was hoping that her sister was listening; and she was deeply worried that Drew wouldn't hear the preacher's message, a message that she obviously needed to hear. Dani worried that Drew was so eager to experience this new life that she wanted so badly that she'd ignore the Holy Spirit and get herself into trouble.

Drew, on the other hand, was sitting quietly, looking at her fingernails, digging in her purse for a piece of gum, staying busy rather than truly listening to the words of the pastor. She had heard enough and, even though she knew that he was technically correct, it wasn't a message that she wanted to hear or was willing to do anything about at that moment.

"Sit up and listen, Drew." Mrs. Daniels

nudged her, trying to get her to take interest in the sermon. "Stop fidgeting so much," she whispered to her daughter.

Drew was very happy when the sermon was over and the congregation rose to their feet to sing a closing chorus. On the way out, they shook the hands of the people they passed; and as they approached the pastor, they paused to say hello. Mr. Daniels shook his hand and said, "Great sermon today, Pastor. You really hit home with this one."

"I'm very glad you got something out of it. How about you, young lady?" Pastor Michaels asked Drew.

She wondered if he had noticed her inattention. "I thought you did a good job, too." Drew didn't quite know what to say.

"Oh, I'm not looking for compliments on my speaking ability. I was wondering if the message reached you in any way."

"Sure, it did. It's important to do what God wants us to do and not only what we want to do," Drew answered, glad that she had heard at least part of the sermon but frustrated to be put on the spot like that.

"It sounds like you did hear something

after all. Just be sure that you take it seriously, young lady. They are nice words, but the truth behind them is what's powerful."

"Yes, sir. Thank you." Drew couldn't wait to escape the scrutiny.

"Man, I feel like I just got into trouble," Drew complained as they walked to the car.

"Drew, it was clear that you weren't paying any attention. I was even a bit embarrassed. Perhaps the pastor sensed that it was a message you needed to hear," Drew's mom suggested.

"I don't know why; I was just bored."

"You still need to respect Pastor Michaels enough that you pay attention and don't become a distraction."

Realizing that she wasn't helping herself at all with her current attitude, Drew relented. "You're right, Mom. Sorry about that."

"It's okay, sweetie. Just make sure you don't do that again. Now where should we go eat?" Mrs. Daniels asked, changing the subject.

"I vote for Shakey's," Dani jumped in, suggesting the pizza buffet.

"Sounds good to me," Drew agreed.

"I'll go for that, too," Dad said.

"Sounds like it's unanimous. Shakey's it is."

They arrived at their favorite restaurant, and, as starved as they were, they were thrilled that it was a buffet so they didn't have to wait for their food to be cooked and brought to their table. As they were being seated, they passed two students from school who were there with their families. They both said hello to Drew but ignored Dani.

Pretending not to notice or care, Dani slid into the booth first, followed by Drew and their parents on the other side. They made several trips to the buffet and enjoyed a leisurely lunch.

"I have news," Dani said.

"News? We've been together all weekend. How could you have something new to tell us that we haven't heard already?" Drew laughed.

"Well, I guess it's more of an announcement than news, so far anyway."

"The suspense is killing me. What is it?" Drew prodded.

"I have decided to try out for the debate team," Dani announced, then sat back in her seat to wait for the comments. She was visibly happy with herself for coming to that decision.

"That's great, sweetheart. When did you decide?" Mrs. Daniels asked.

"Ever since we talked about it the other

day, I haven't been able to stop thinking about it. I just think it's something I would be good at and I would enjoy. Plus, like Dad said, it will only help my college transcripts."

"I'm all for it," Mr. Daniels encouraged. "And I do think you'll be terrific at it."

"That's awesome, sis. I think it definitely is your thing. When are tryouts? Can we be there?"

"Aw, thanks for even wanting to be. . . ," Dani began but was interrupted by Drew.

"Of course we want to support you. I can't wait to come watch you argue with people. It'll be awesome." Drew laughed.

They're Tuesday after school. I almost missed them, so it's a really good thing that we discussed it when we did. I had to dig up the calendar of events that we got when school started. Now I just have to practice as much as possible before then. Do you guys want to help me practice, maybe?"

"Definitely. How do you practice for that, though?" Drew wondered.

"I looked online at the types of categories and contests that are part of a typical debate-team event. The one that sounds the most interesting to me are debates where you have to blindly select a controversial category, like legalizing drugs, for example, and begin to argue one side of the debate. Then, when the bell rings, you have to flip and argue the other side—all with no preparation. Then you're scored for how persuasive you were on both sides of the argument. Talk about thinking on your feet." Dani laughed. "So maybe you guys could pick some topics and then help me figure out how to formulate arguments for the multiple sides of the debate. What do you think?"

Everyone agreed that it sounded like fun and even kind of fascinating. They all agreed to help that evening and Monday night, as well.

"This is going to be a fun year for us," Mrs. Daniels said to her husband. "These girls are going to keep us busy with their activities, but at least they are both so very interesting."

"Oh, I completely agree. It's going to be a great year. We should learn a lot from these two." Both parents laughed at the thought.

Chapter 7

FAMOUS LAST WORDS

"Drew, phone for you," Mr. Daniels called up the stairs. "Who's calling, please?" he asked the person on the other line while he was waiting for Drew to pick up.

"My name is Trevor, sir. I go to school with Drew."

"Hello, Trevor. Have we met?" Mr. Daniels asked him.

"No, sir, but I look forward to meeting you," Trevor said politely just as they heard a *click* on the other end of the phone line.

"Dad, I'm on the phone now. You can hang up," Drew impatiently said from the upstairs phone. Once her dad had hung up the receiver, Drew excitedly said, "Trevor, it's great to hear from you. What's going on?"

"Oh, nothing much. I was just thinking about how much fun we had the other night, and I thought I'd give you a call to see if you were thinking the same thing," Trevor admitted.

"Yeah, to be honest, I haven't thought about much else since."

"Me, too." Neither of them was used to being so open and vulnerable and, though it felt good and very grown-up, it was a little awkward, and a few moments of silence followed.

"So what have you been doing today, Drew?"

"I went to church with my family and then out to eat lunch. Just now Dani and I were in our room working on homework. How about you?"

"I slept in until about eleven, and I've been playing video games since I got up. Just kind of a lazy day."

"Sometimes those are the best kind of days, especially after a night like Friday."

"I agree, and at least I didn't have to get up to go to church. Do you have to go every Sunday?"

"Yeah, believe it or not, we go every

Sunday morning and every Wednesday night, too. But Wednesday night is for youth group, which is fun."

"Man, I don't know if I could take that much church. I'm lucky that my parents don't make us go. Do you hate it?"

"No, I wouldn't say I hate it. I sure would have preferred to sleep in this morning, though." Drew laughed and then felt a little guilty for not standing up for her family's values and supporting her church rather than almost mocking it with her comments. She wasn't sure what to say next to repair her previous statements. She decided a change in subjects was a good idea. "So, do you have any brothers or sisters, Trevor?"

"I have two little brothers and one little sister. My sister is almost two years old, and the boys are in between."

"That's a lot of kids." Drew laughed. "Do you like having little kids around or is it a pain?"

"It's not so bad. . .sometimes. It definitely has its moments. You'll have to meet them someday soon."

"I'd love to meet them."

Neither of the teens was very practiced in these types of conversations, so another slightly awkward silence followed. Drew twisted the phone cord between her fingers until Trevor spoke up again.

"So, you have a twin sister, huh?" When Drew said yes, he went on. "Is that weird? I mean, what's it like to have someone who looks just like you?"

"It's pretty cool. I mean, my sister will always be my best friend. But even though we look alike, we have different personalities and interests. We're just now starting to figure that out and do some things separately. Before, we did everything exactly the same."

"Do people ever get you mixed up?"

"Yeah, that used to happen a lot. It doesn't happen as much since I changed my hair, and I think that we just act differently lately."

"Did you ever try to mix people up?"

"Oh, yeah. We've had lots of fun with that. We used to go to each other's classes and try to mix up the teachers. It almost always worked. Once in a while we'd slip up and get caught. It was always funny, though." Drew laughed at the memory. "One time, at summer Bible camp, we spent the whole week messing people up just for fun. We would switch beds and change our clothes midday. It was definitely a diversion in what had been kind of a boring week other than that."

"Well, at the risk of you two doing that to me, I'll take my chances and ask if you want to go on a real date with me on Saturday night," Trevor asked with a nervous tremor.

Drew laughed out loud. "Oh don't worry, I wouldn't trick you like that, and I don't think it would work anymore, anyway. But of course, I'd love to go out with you on Saturday," Drew answered, not telling him that she wouldn't be allowed to go on a date. She was determined to find a way to get permission. "I'll let you know in school tomorrow, just so I can make sure that my family doesn't have any other plans. Otherwise, it would be perfect."

"Great. I have to run for now, though," Trevor said. "So, I'll see you in school tomorrow?"

"You bet. Thanks for calling."

Drew hung up the phone and sat quietly for a moment, contemplating the conversation she just had. The cutest and most popular boy in school had just called her and asked her out on a date. But her parents would never let her go, she realized with a sinking feeling.

Drew considered all of her options. Maybe they would let her go if it were a group of kids—no, she quickly dismissed that idea. Even the idea of a group date would be quickly rejected by her parents. Maybe if she were honest with Trevor and invited him over to her house, they would get to have their "date" and her parents would get a chance to get to know him—no, that wouldn't work, either. Then she would have to admit to Trevor that she wasn't allowed to date. Drew wondered how she could ever avoid him knowing that. She finally realized that she may just need some more time to ease into this and get her parents on her side, so she hoped that they had plans for Saturday night. Friday night would be game night and Sunday night was a school night; so if she could just get out of her "date" with Trevor for Saturday night, then she'd have a whole week before next weekend to work something out—which she fully intended to do.

"Dani, we need to talk. I need your help," Drew announced as she walked back into their bedroom and flopped on her own bed across the room from her sister.

Dani looked up from the book that she was reading and raised her eyebrows in question. "What's up?"

"Trevor asked me to go out on a date with him on Saturday night."

"I don't know how I can help with *that.*" Dani frowned as she put her book down. "You know it's not going to happen. Besides, we have plans for Saturday night. It's Grandma's birthday, remember?"

"It is?" Drew practically shouted in relief. "That's great!"

"How is that great? I thought you were happy he asked you out."

"Oh, I'm happy, that's for sure. But I think I need more time to figure out how to get permission."

"Drew. . ." Dani leaned forward and lowered her voice in seriousness. "What's the big deal? Why do you want to rush it so much? Why not just leave it alone?"

"You just don't understand. Trevor is the cutest boy in school, probably the most popular, too. Going out with him would really help me make a name for myself."

"You don't need *him* to make a name for

yourself. . .whatever that means. You're awesome all by yourself."

"I want more, Dani. You just don't understand."

"I get that you think you want something 'more,' but I just don't understand what that means. More of what?"

"I want to be popular. I want to have tons of friends. I want recognition and for people to know my name. I want to be prom queen one day. This is all part of making those plans a reality."

"So, poor Trevor is just a way for you to get the popularity you want? Is that fair to him?"

"It's not like that. I really do like him. Have you seen how cute he is? He is totally fun and has a great sense of humor, too. Plus, I like the way it feels when he holds my hand."

"What? He held your hand?" Dani was shocked her sister would have let things go so far with a boy she hardly knew. "Oh, Drew, this is going so fast. You really need to think about what you're doing."

"I have everything under control. Don't worry about me." Drew patted Dani on her leg as she got up to leave the room. She realized that

Dani just wasn't ready for the changes that Drew was experiencing.

"Famous last words, Drew. Famous last words."

Chapter 8

PEP RALLY

"Oh, how cute you look." Mrs. Daniels grinned when she saw Drew dressed for school on Monday morning. It was Pep-Rally Monday, which was a tradition for the third week of school. It was a way to recognize the football team and cheerleaders and build school spirit and team support. As part of the event, it was an unspoken understanding that the players and cheerleaders would wear their home-game uniforms to school for the day.

Drew was so excited about it, which was obvious by her big grin as she bounced into the kitchen. She was wearing her short-sleeved, tight, white cheerleading top that said PANTHERS down the right side with a gold and red chevron on the chest. The little cheerleading skirt was the shortest skirt Drew had ever worn. Brick red with gold cording around the hem, it flounced around her upper thighs as she swayed through the room. Her clean, white sneakers and white ankle socks finished off the outfit. Her hair was tied back in a ponytail and secured with a gold ribbon, and she was wearing the extra make-up that her parents agreed she could wear for cheering events, unaware that she wore it every day, anyway. Drew was the perfect picture of a wholesome athlete, and her smile proved her happiness.

"This is going to be such a fun day. You're still going to come, right, Mom?"

"Of course, honey. I wouldn't miss it for the world. I'll be at the school by one thirty to get a good seat. Now, you'd better eat something and get ready to go before you're late. Where's your sister?"

"Dani says she doesn't feel good. She's dressed, but she says she isn't going to school."

"What? Really? I'd better go check on her." Mrs. Daniels left in a hurry to check on her daughter. She was sure that illness wasn't really Dani's problem.

A few minutes later, Dani and her mom were walking into the kitchen, smiling. Whatever had been ailing Dani must have passed, because she looked just fine to Drew. "You ready, sis? Big day today. We need to go." Drew was so excited she could hardly contain her energy.

Drew spent a few minutes talking with Trevor in the hallway before first period. But just as quickly as they had started chatting, the bell rang, signaling that they had two minutes to be in their seats for their first class. "Oops, better run. I'll catch you at the pep rally later."

"You bet," Drew said. "See you then." They turned and ran off in separate directions to their classes. They didn't share any classes because they were two years apart. They did luck out and get the same lunch hour, though. But Drew wouldn't see Trevor for lunch that day because the football team was having a pre-rally meeting. So she was on her own until later. Racing through the hall to get to her class, Drew could tell that the other girls were looking at her with envy, and the boys were looking her up and down, checking out how she looked in her cheerleading uniform. This had to be the best day ever, Drew decided.

"Hey, Drew. How's it going?" Sam, one of the varsity cheerleaders she met at The Grill last Friday night, slid into the seat next to her just before the bell rang. They had their homeroom class first, which was the perfect time to finish up homework from the day before, study for any tests or quizzes that would be given that day, or to quietly chitchat with a neighbor. But that day, Drew was too riled up to settle down to schoolwork, so she welcomed Sam's company.

"I'm great. You ready for the pep rally?" Drew asked

"Oh yeah, it's going to be so cool. You look great today, by the way." When Drew thanked her, she continued. "So, I hear you and Trevor have become a hot item."

"News travels fast, doesn't it?"

"So it's true? You're together now?" Sam seemed impressed.

"I suppose so. He's asked me out on a date, and he wants to hang out all of the time. I don't know that I would say that anything is official, though."

"What a major development for freshman

year. Way to go."

Drew, proud of herself but wanting to stay cool, answered, "Well, we'll see. He still has to pass a few tests."

"Are you kidding me? He's perfect. What tests could you possibly be talking about?"

"Oh, I don't know. I haven't thought of them yet." Drew laughed at her admission. "I'm pretty much kidding. He is kind of perfect, isn't he?" The girls dissolved into fits of giggles until their teacher reminded them to keep it down.

The cheerleading coach was grinning from ear to ear as she got her squads ready for the pep rally. "Girls, this is going to be a phenomenal year. It's one of those times when everything has just fallen into place and it makes magic. Our football teams are so talented and stand a great chance of making it to the championships, the cheerleading squads are the most talented and creative teams I've ever had the privilege of coaching, and the school and community are energized and behind us like never before. That gymnasium is packed with people from throughout the community who have come here today to soak in *your* spirit. You girls, more than anyone else, drive the energy and the spirit that supports our teams and our schools. You need to go out there today with nothing on your mind other than getting energy from that crowd. Are you ready, girls?"

Every girl let out a shout of excitement, each one ready to not only raise school spirit but also to soak it in from the crowd. Drew's heart was beating so fast; she was eager but nervous.

Finally, the double doors to the gym opened, and the cheerleaders were introduced first. The JV team was brought out before the varsity team. Each girl was introduced by name, at which time she would come into the gym, running the length of the gym floor, shaking her pom-poms and waving to the crowds in the bleachers that lined both sides of the gym. One by one, each girl had her moment to shine in front of the crowd. Drew was introduced last for her team. "And last, but certainly not least, we want you to meet our junior varsity squad captain, Drew Daniels!"

When she heard her name, Drew took off running toward the middle of the gym floor, did a round-off, a back flip, and then turned and waved her pom-poms at the crowd with a big grin on her face. She was a natural, and the crowd loved her energy and her big, beautiful smile. She soaked it all in and then jogged over to the side where her team was lined up.

The varsity team was introduced in the same way, and those cheerleaders lined up on the other side of the gymnasium. The two teams formed two parallel lines and waited for the big moment—the entrance of the football team. Each player was introduced, and they ran through the lines of cheerleaders to the sounds of cheering, shouting, jumping, and bouncing. The players really seemed buoyed by the experience, and the crowd loved every second of it.

When the introductions were over, the band started to play the school song and the cheerleaders got into formation and did their signature dance and cheer. The crowd went wild over the cool moves and the huge smiles.

In the stands, Dani was sitting with her mom and dad. They were thoroughly enjoying themselves and cheering right along with the rest of the crowd.

"I really had no idea it would be like this," Mrs. Daniels said. "Drew is going to have so many great high school memories if she sticks with this." Mrs. Daniels snapped picture after picture of the celebration.

"Oh, believe me, she'll be sticking with it." Dani wondered if her mom would be so excited for Drew if she knew how serious Drew was getting about a boy—the captain of the football team, no less. Somehow, she doubted it.

Drew and her team moved to the sidelines and cheered as the coaches were introduced. Trevor came to stand by her while the coaches gave rousing speeches meant to continue stirring the crowd. Trevor and Drew stood together and looked comfortable together, like they had known each other for a long time. Dani wondered if her parents were noticing, but she was afraid to look for fear of drawing attention to them.

But when Trevor leaned down to whisper something in Drew's ear, Dani couldn't stand it any longer. She tried to look out of the corner of her eye at her mom. Dani's mom slowly lowered the camera to her lap, and she leaned forward a bit. Her mouth was slightly open, and her eyes were wide in surprise. She nudged her husband, nodded toward the scene she was witnessing, and raised her eyebrows in question, wondering if he saw the same thing she did.

"Dani, who is that boy your sister is talking to?" Mrs. Daniels asked.

"That's Trevor Jaymes. He's the captain of the football team."

"Oh, he's the boy who called the other day, isn't he?" Mr. Daniels asked.

"Is he a freshman, too?" Mrs. Daniels hoped so, even though it was clear that he was not.

"No, he's a junior, Mom. He's a nice guy, though."

"I'm sure he is. . . ." Mrs. Daniels didn't ask any further questions at that time, but Dani knew that they would stew in her head and she would have a lot to ask Drew later. Dani hoped she wouldn't be around for that conversation.

Down on the floor, Trevor was asking Drew if she wanted to be his girlfriend. He understood that with their schedules there wouldn't be much time for actual dates; but they would have a lot of time together due to their athletic activities, and they would fit private dates in wherever they could.

Drew beamed with pride and excitement. "Of course I want to be your girlfriend, Trevor. I really like being with you, and I think this year is going to be a blast."

"Great. It's settled then." As a joke, he held up his hand for a high five.

She laughed and slapped his hand with a flourish. She was glad he didn't try to seal the deal with a kiss or something. That was definitely not something she wanted to experience for the first time on a crowded gym floor in front of hundreds of people—including her parents.

It was six o'clock before Drew got home after practice that evening. She was eager to hear what her family had to say about the rally. It had been way too crowded and noisy to try to find them to chat after the rally was over, but she was sure they'd have a lot to say now. She was also a little nervous to find out if her parents had seen anything when she and Trevor were talking on the sidelines. Maybe it would be a good thing, a way to ease them into the idea. She knew, though, that she'd have to be careful how hard she pushed them at first. They would need time to get used to the idea.

"Hi, everyone, I'm home!" Drew announced as she walked into the house after practice. When she arrived at the entryway to the kitchen, she said, "Wow, Mom. It smells so good in here. I'm completely famished."

"I figured you would be. I made your favorite—manicotti and garlic bread."

"Oh, that's awesome. Let's eat!"

Over dinner, they were abuzz about the day's goings-on. "Drew, I have to tell you, I was so proud of you today. I'm so excited for the experience you're going to have in high school," Mrs. Daniels said.

"Me, too," Mr. Daniels said. "I had a good time at the rally, and I think it's wonderful how much school spirit and support is behind your teams. It's inspiring. I'm still not thrilled with those short skirts," he admitted. "But you did look great out there—a real natural."

"Thanks, Mom and Dad. I can't believe how much fun I'm having with it all. I really feel like I'm doing what I was meant to be doing right now."

"That much is clear." Mrs. Daniels paused to take a drink of her milk to wash down her food. "There's something else that was clear, too."

Drew groaned inwardly, knowing what was coming. "What's that, Mom?" She feigned innocence.

"It's pretty clear that you and that boy we saw you with have a bit of a crush on each other."

"Who? Trevor?" Drew tried to act shocked, but her mom wasn't buying it.

"You know who I mean. That dreamy boy who was talking to you like there was no one else around. What's the deal there?"

"Well, I guess a crush is a good way to put it. You know how it goes, captain of the football team and cheerleading captain—it's kind of a natural thing."

"It may very well be," her mom said, "but you are quite a bit younger than him. You aren't ready for a relationship like he may be."

Drew shot her sister a look, knowing that Dani must have told Mom how old he was.

Dad, having been quiet until then, jumped in. "I agree, Drew. You are too young to be in a relationship, and you are in the middle of so many other changes right now. Take it one thing at a time."

"It's not like I'm asking to be allowed to go on dates or anything," Drew argued.

"Then what are you asking? Or what are you planning?"

"We just like each other. Neither of us

really has time for dates or outside things, so we're just enjoying the fact that we share our team athletics. I am in high school now, and this is part of it. There will probably be other boys as time goes on."

"If that's all it is, I can probably understand that," Mom said. "But don't think it's going to turn into you going on private dates. That won't be happening until you're sixteen, and you know that."

"I know, Mom. What about school-sponsored activities like dances and stuff like that?"

"Oh, that's different. Of course you may go to dances like homecoming and prom. That's all part of getting the full experience of high school; plus, they are chaperoned activities."

Feeling like she had made huge strides, Drew decided that she had better quit while she was ahead. "May I be excused now? I really need to shower, and then I have homework to do." With her parent's agreement, Drew excused herself from the table and headed off for the shower, where she'd have a few moments to herself to daydream about all that had taken place that day. It was a day for the history books.

Chapter 9

INVISIBLE

Dani felt invisible when she was with Drew. Everywhere they went they were met with choruses of, "Hi, Drew." "I like your hair, Drew." "That's a cute shirt, Drew." Everyone seemed to want to talk to Drew and be her friend. They all knew her name, even though Drew knew only a handful of them.

It was much like any celebrity status, Dani realized; people just wanted to make a connection, no matter how small.

Drew squealed next to Dani, making her jump, as Trevor sneaked up behind her and covered her eyes with his hands, saying, "Guess who!"

"I know who it is, silly." Drew giggled and Dani rolled her eyes.

"You'd better know who it is. I mean, everyone else better keep his hands off," Trevor teased possessively, making Drew smile even wider.

"Hi, Dani. How are you today?" he asked, trying to include Dani.

"Oh, I'm fine, thanks. You?"

"Just fine, now that I've seen my girl."

"I have to run to class. I'll see you two later." Dani scurried off, mainly just to get away from the syrupy sweetness of young love that she was tired of enduring. As an afterthought, she turned to Drew and said, "It's Tuesday, so wait for me out front after school, okay?"

"As always, sis. See ya then," Drew promised, forgetting for a moment why Tuesday was different than any other day.

"Finally, a moment alone," Trevor teased, because they were never really alone. Everywhere they went, their friends and other kids wanted their attention. Both of them loved it, though. They seemed made for each other and everyone saw it.

Though he didn't want to leave Drew,

Trevor couldn't afford to be late to class, since the coach always checked up on that. "I'd better get going, too. See you at lunch?"

"Of course. Save me a seat, okay?" Drew had farther to walk to the lunchroom, so Trevor always got there before she did. For a second she considered asking him to save a seat for Dani but then dismissed the idea because she didn't think that Dani would want to sit with Trevor and his friends. It was just not her thing.

Racing to the lunchroom so she'd have as much time as possible, Drew got there in record time. She spotted Trevor and his friends in their usual spot and waved across the room. On her way to meet him, she passed by the table she used to share with her sister, who was already sitting in her favorite seat. "Here ya go, Drew." She patted the seat next to her as Drew was about to breeze past.

"Oh. . .Dani. . .I thought you realized. . . I'll be eating lunch at Trevor's table from now on." Drew nervously chewed on the side of her fingernail. She didn't want to hurt Dani, but she was sure it was inevitable. "You're welcome to join us."

"I just didn't think. Of course you'll be eating with Trevor. . .I guess it just didn't click." Dani looked fine about what she was saying, but Drew knew her inside and out. Dani was crushed. It was a sad realization that she would be eating relatively alone from now on. Sure, there were other people who would be around, friends of theirs she could talk to, girls to joke around with while she ate her lunch. But the loss of the presence of the other half of her heart made the remaining half feel broken.

Drew pretended to believe that Dani was fine with it all and headed over to sit with Trevor. Somehow, though, her excitement had diminished and the sparkle was dimmed because she knew that she had disappointed her sister. Drew managed to put her guilt aside as soon as she saw how happy the group was to see her. She, a new freshman, was eating lunch at the table where all of the star football players and varsity cheerleaders ate. She beamed with pride while trying to maintain her composure so they wouldn't know how excited she actually was.

"Hey, there's my girl," Trevor said above

the loud lunchroom noises.

"Hey, you. I'm famished.What's for lunch today?" Drew asked, sliding into the seat beside Trevor.

Sam informed her that the hot lunch was beef tips and noodles but that she wouldn't eat something so fattening, so she was just having the salad option.

"Yeah, that's a good idea. I sure don't want those extra calories either." In reality, Drew would have loved the beef and noodles; it was one of her favorite hot lunches. But she surely didn't want the group to think she wasn't watching her weight. She went to the lunch counter and came back with a side salad and dinner roll, hoping it would tide her over until she got home that afternoon.

Lunch was a party of laughter and chatting. The time went too fast for Drew. While she did enjoy herself immensely, the whole thing was bittersweet as she watched her sister sit quietly across the lunchroom. Drew wondered for a moment if she had made a mistake. She didn't want to choose her new friends over her sister. But then again, she reasoned, she shouldn't be forced to. Her sister should want her to do the things that made her happy and to meet new people.

"Meet me after school outside the sports office?" Trevor whispered to Drew before they broke to head to their afternoon classes.

"I don't think I can stay long. I have to meet Dani right after school today, but I can't remember why. I could meet you for a few minutes, though," Drew offered.

"A few minutes is all I need." Trevor smiled suggestively, making Drew wonder what he was up to.

She laughed and said, "I can't figure you out half the time. But all right, I'll meet you there right after school for a few minutes." She waved at the rest of the group as they all headed off in their separate directions. She had hoped to break away with enough time to see Dani before class, but Dani was already gone. Drew sighed and hoped that she could make it up to her at home later.

The final bell rang, signaling the end of the school day. Drew hurriedly gathered her books and things and headed for her locker. She shoved everything in there, only keeping the one book that she needed for homework, grabbed her purse, and hurried for the sports office, eager to find out why Trevor wanted to see her.

Walking down the corridor toward the sports office, Drew smiled and realized that she would be spending a lot of time in that corridor over the next four years. Spotting Trevor talking to his coach, Drew hung back for a moment, giving them space. As soon as he saw her, though, he broke away from his conversation, clapping the coach on the back, and headed over to her immediately. "I know you only have a couple of minutes, so let's not waste a moment's time."

"Sounds good to me, I think. Where are we going?"

"Follow me." He grabbed her hand and headed toward the exit that led to the football field. They walked quickly onto the field and then climbed into the bleachers.

After climbing all the way to the top of the bleachers, he pulled her down to the seat beside him. "Look out there." Trevor pointed to the empty football field. "Have you ever seen it like this?" When Drew shook her head no, he continued. "I love seeing it empty like this. It reminds me of how big it really is. It's amazing to me that it sits here lonely like this until we come and bring it to life. It really gets me charged up."

"Oh, I can see what you're saying. What a beautiful thought. You really can't get the feel of the place when it's full of people in the stands and players on the field. It's nice to sit back and get to know the personality of it when it's alone."

"That's exactly how I feel about it. It's alive."

Drew smiled and sighed as she looked around the empty field. She looked from one end of the field, through the bleachers on the other side, and past the goal posts on the other end of the field, around back to where they were seated. Once she had her fill of the sights, she looked at Trevor, only to realize that he was looking at her. She blushed when she realized he had been looking at her the whole time.

Trevor smiled at her and cupped her chin in his hand and leaned toward her. Drew realized that he intended to kiss her. This was about to be her first kiss. It was probably under the perfect circumstances; but she also wasn't really ready for it. Still, she wanted Trevor to kiss her, and she wouldn't dream of telling him not to.

As all of those thoughts sailed through her mind, he leaned in toward her lips. She should probably do her part and meet him halfway so that he wouldn't think she didn't want the kiss.

Palms sweating, cheeks on fire, she leaned toward Trevor. Their lips met in a soft, quick kiss. Just as quickly, they both backed away. She was thankful that it was a quick kiss. It was all she could handle.

Flushed and breathless, they looked at each other for a moment and Drew began to giggle.

Trevor laughed and said, "You've really gotten to me, Drew Daniels. I never expected to get serious about someone this year."

"You've gotten to me, too. Believe me," Drew assured him. "I'm really glad, though."

Knowing that it was time for Drew to head home, they got up from their seats and retraced their steps back through the building. At the school's entrance, Trevor squeezed Drew's hand and said that he would see her tomorrow. She smiled and turned to walk in the direction of her house. Not riding the bus, like she sometimes did, would mean a long walk alone. Immediately she saw the spot where she normally met her sister.

With horror, Drew remembered that she had told Dani that she would meet her there after school so they could walk home together. She had never told Dani that she wouldn't be there.

With a backward glance over her shoulder at Trevor, she smiled and waved again, then headed quickly for home. Worried about how her sister was feeling, she jogged part of the way.

What a day. She had dropped the bomb on Dani that they wouldn't be eating lunch together anymore and then completely blew her off after school. Dani was probably at home, feeling very left out and lonely. Drew knew that's how she would feel if the roles were reversed.

But on the other hand, should Drew be stuck only doing what Dani wanted to do? Didn't Drew have the right to make new friends and have new experiences? She spent the remainder of the walk trying to convince herself, against nagging doubts, that she had done nothing wrong when it came to her treatment of Dani. She also hoped that Dani wasn't mad enough at her to tell Mom all that had been going on. Realizing that was a real risk, Drew promised herself that she would be much more careful in the future.

Tentatively walking into the house, Drew cautiously called out Dani's name. She wasn't sitting on the couch watching TV where Drew had expected she would be.

"Dani?" Drew called hesitantly and softly as she climbed the stairs toward their room. "We need to talk. . . . Dani? Dani?" Drew poked her head in every room, looking for her sister, but it was clear that she was nowhere to be found. Drew started to worry and considered calling Mom on her cell phone. Before she did anything, though, she needed to wash her makeup off.

Back in the family room, after scrubbing her face, Drew sat down on the couch to think things through. Where could Dani be? Why hadn't she come home? Or had she come home and left? Should Drew call one of their parents?

She walked into the kitchen to see if Dani's backpack was where she normally dropped it when she got home. No backpack, so Drew assumed that Dani hadn't come home at all yet. Where could she be?

Suddenly, the realization hit her. Today

was the day of Dani's tryout for the debate team. They had been working with her to prepare for days. How could she have forgotten? Dani was going to be crushed, and her parents would likely be angry. Oh man, she really did it this time.

At about that time, Drew heard the garage door opening. Trying to look casual, she got a quick glass of milk and sat at the kitchen table. When they walked in, Drew said, "Hey, guys. How did it go? I'm so sorry I couldn't make it."

Dani wouldn't even look at Drew as she hurried out of the kitchen and went upstairs. But not before Drew noticed that Dani's eyes were bloodshot; she had been crying. The pain was evident in Dani's sad eyes. It broke Drew's heart when she realized how much Dani was hurting.

"Mom. . .I. . .what can I say? What can I do? I'm so sorry. I forgot to let Dani know that I wouldn't be able to meet her after school. It doesn't mean anything. I just had something come up for cheerleading that I needed to do." Drew felt bad about lying, but she didn't think she had a choice. She didn't want to hurt her sister even more with the truth.

"Drew, you need to talk to your sister. This isn't something I can fix for you. And next time something comes up like that, you need to call home and let someone know where you'll be and what time you'll be home. Okay?"

Drew agreed and apologized for the oversight; and then, eager to talk to Dani, she left the kitchen and went upstairs to find Dani crying softly on her bed.

"Dani, I'm so sorry. I'm sorry I couldn't be there, and I'm sorry that the tryout didn't go well."

"You *could* have been there, but you chose not to be. Don't think I didn't see you in the bleachers with Trevor. You picked him over me again. . .and on such an important day. You have no idea how much that hurt, still hurts actually."

"To be honest, Dani, I forgot about it for a little bit after school. It wasn't like I made a conscious choice to ignore you and your needs."

"Drew, this goes so much deeper than just forgetting me after school. It's about the fact that you are slowly pulling away from everything having anything to do with me, and it just doesn't seem to bother you one bit. You don't even miss me."

Dani's words cut like a knife. Drew knew that Dani was right, and she didn't know what to say to make her feel better.

"Dani, it's just that I don't believe that we, or I, can't have both. Why can't we have our relationship *and* I can have a boyfriend and a commitment to a sport? Why does being your sister mean that's all I can have?"

"No, Drew, you've got it all wrong. Loyalty is the issue here. It's not about having it all—you could have it all without even trying. Instead, you have chosen that other stuff over me and pushed me aside without any consideration of my feelings. It's not that you want 'both,' it's that you want me to step aside and let you do your own thing until you decide you need me again. The sad thing is, I'll do that. I'll be here—I'm not going anywhere. But I can't pretend it doesn't hurt."

Drew was speechless, but tears began to form in her eyes. She never wanted to hurt Dani like she had.

"I was worried when you didn't show up, so I went looking for you. I saw your first kiss. Funny, that was something that I thought we would discuss and share with each other. I thought we would squeal and jump up and down and run upstairs to our room where we could dissect every single detail. But at this point,

Drew, I don't even want to know about it. That is what I had to think about the whole time I was trying out for the debate team, which is as important to me as your cheerleading is to you. By the way, what makes you think that my tryout went badly?"

Drew said, "I haven't seen you so sad in a long time, so I assumed that you didn't make the team."

"Oh, I made the team all right. It's the fact that I couldn't share it with you that broke my heart." Dani abruptly stood and started to leave the room. On her way to the stairs, she turned and looked hard at Drew. "I sure hope you know what you're doing."

Chapter 10

WHAT THEY DON'T KNOW

Drew missed Dani. Sure, they still shared a room and walked to school together, but their relationship ended there all week. Drew was busy after school with long practices every day, so Dani walked home alone after her shorter debate team practices. During school, Drew spent every spare second with Trevor, so Dani hung out with other people. At lunchtime, Drew sat with Trevor and his friends, so Dani ate with her other friends across the room. It was a sad week for Dani, and even for Drew in many ways. But mostly, Drew was enjoying her life and missed only certain things—things that she was more than willing to sacrifice.

Fridays were always supercharged with energy because there was usually a football game that night. When it was an away game, the teams wore their white uniforms with red and gold accents to school on Friday. Home games were the best, though. The community turned out in support, and, together with hundreds of students, they showed their spirit in so many ways. When it was a home game, they wore the red uniforms with the white and gold accents to school that day. Drew loved wearing her uniform to school; it made her feel really important.

As Drew was putting her books into her locker, Trevor sneaked up behind her and put his arm around her neck and gave a playful squeeze.

"Hey, there, silly. How are you today?" She looked him up and down in approval and he did the same.

"You look great," they said to each other simultaneously and then laughed.

"Are we going to eat and party after the game tonight?"

"I hope so. I'll have to check with my parents."

Trevor rolled his eyes. "Come on, they

need to get with the times and understand that you've got things to do." He laughed at his teasing, but Drew could also tell that he didn't like to be put off by such immature things as needing permission.

"Oh come on, you know how it is. They just have trouble letting go of their little girl. I'm sure you had a curfew when you were a freshman, too." Drew laughed good-naturedly.

"That's not really the point. You know, Drew, I'm not used to dating a freshman; I'm sort of past all of that needing permission stuff. I hope this isn't going to be a problem. I mean, I want to have my girl with me when I celebrate, not have to have her home and in bed by ten o'clock or some other crazy curfew."

Drew was slightly annoyed by his lack of understanding but didn't want to let him see that. "I'll do the best I can, Trevor. I hope I can work it out."

"Parents don't need to know everything. You don't have to say that you want to spend time with your boyfriend and that it's a date. Just tell them it's a school event and that everyone goes out after the game. Or even better, tell them you're spending the night at a friend's house.

That way we can stay out later. You could stay at Samantha's after our date."

"She hasn't invited me, though," Drew protested.

"Oh, don't worry about that at all. She does this all the time."

"Okay. I'll think about it. Don't worry about it, though. I'll figure it out. We'll definitely go out after the game."

"Good. That's my girl. I've got to run to class or I'll be late. See you!"

Drew smiled as he ran down the hall, dodging bodies along the way like any good quarterback would do. No matter how far away he got, Drew could still see his tall frame and broad shoulders above the crowd. Smiling and lost in thought, she finished collecting her books and went to class, thinking about how she would get permission to go out with the gang after the game.

"Drew! You're going to be late. Let's go!" Mrs. Daniels called up the stairs to let Drew know that it was time to leave for the game. She had rushed home from school to shower and get dressed in her uniform in preparation of their second home game. She was so excited about the game but also nervous about getting the permission she needed to go out afterward.

Skipping down the stairs, dark ponytail bouncing with each step, Drew said, "Here I come, Mom. Is everyone else ready?"

"Yep, we're all waiting. Let's go."

On the way there, Mrs. Daniels said, "After the game, I think we should all go out for ice cream to celebrate."

"Um, that's a good idea. . .but I sort of thought I would ask if I could make other plans." Drew hesitantly broached the subject of her "date."

"What were you hoping to do tonight, Drew?" Mr. Daniels jumped in with concern.

"Oh, it's no big deal. It's just that the teams usually go out to The Grill after games, and it's such a fun thing to be a part of. I was hoping that I'd be able to make that a part of my game-night ritual—at least for home games."

"Well, let us think about it, and we'll talk about it after the game," Mrs. Daniels suggested.

"Okay, Mom. That's fine." Drew didn't want to argue, because she knew it wouldn't do any good; but she really had hoped to have this worked out before the game. No matter. . .she'd figure it out after the game. Maybe spending the night at Sam's would be the best idea. Ignoring feelings of guilt, she tried to refocus her thoughts on the game.

The game was exciting. The crowd was wild and the players were doing great. By halftime, they were winning by fourteen points. It was dark by that time, and the stadium lights gave the whole atmosphere a completely different feel. The halftime show was perfectly executed and generated enough buzz in the crowd to get the team through the second half. Drew loved every minute of it. After the performance, there were some other things taking place on the field, so Trevor and Drew had a few moments to chat.

"Hey, you. You looked really hot out there," Trevor said with a big grin on his face.

"You aren't so bad yourself." Drew winked at him.

"I wanted to tell you, instead of going to The Grill, there's a huge party tonight. It happens to be at Sam's house. She has a big pool and a field behind her house where we'll have a bonfire. We'll go there instead. It's going to be awesome. And Sam said there was no problem with you spending the night. She even said that her older sister would vouch for you if your mom wanted to talk to her *mom*."

"That sounds terrific." Drew's stomach turned at the lies she would have to tell in order to make the date with Trevor. Not to mention the trouble she would get into if she got caught. But the thought of not going was just as upsetting to her. She only had the second half of the game to decide what she was going to do.

It was an agonizing hour and a half as Drew's mind filled with all of the reasons why she didn't want to do it, countered with tons of reasons why she did. She dreaded the thought of lying to her parents and also felt a nudge in her spirit that reminded her of how much this went against what God would want her to do.

She wanted to be a part of all that was going on, and she really believed that she should be allowed to go. She rationalized that her parents would let her spend the night at Samantha's, so that wasn't a lie. And it wasn't really up to her who else Sam invited to her house. . .then again,

Drew's mom and dad would never let her go if they knew there wouldn't be an adult there. If she got caught lying and breaking so many rules, she would surely be grounded for a long time and not be given permission for things like this for a long, long time. However, if she didn't get caught and it worked out great, she would have catapulted her popularity and proven to Trevor that she was fun to be with and willing to make spending time with him a priority, no matter what.

Drew couldn't remember a time when she was so torn over a decision. She had finally gotten to the point where she just wasn't going to go. After all, nothing good should be that difficult. Just as her thoughts had begun to swing in that direction, Trevor came jogging off the field and went in for a drink of water.

He stopped for a minute to talk to Drew and told her, "Drew, you're the cutest thing I've ever seen." He chuckled and continued, "You completely distract me out there. I really hope you are able to come with me tonight. I just want you by my side; I like being close to you."

His words melted her and made her tremble. No one had ever talked to her like that, and it was a heady feeling to be liked so much by the coolest boy in school. She was more confused than ever after that. Wishing she had more time to decide, she went out onto the field to lead the squad in cheering the team on to the end of the game and another victory. After the celebratory lap around the field and the handshakes and high fives with the other team, it was her moment of truth.

IT'S DECISION TIME!

The time has come for you to make your decision. Think long and hard about what you would really do if you were faced with the decision that Drew is facing. It's easy to say that you'd make the right choice. But are you sure that you could stand up to your boyfriend and face his rejection? Once your decision is made, turn to the corresponding page in this book to see how it turns out for Drew—and for you.

Turn to page 130 if Drew is able to stand up to Trevor by not going to the party.

Turn to page 160 if Drew is unable to avoid the temptation and gives in to what Trevor wants her to do.

The next three chapters tell the story of what happened to Drew when she decided to do what she knew was right.

Chapter 11

GONE TOO FAR

Drew knew what she had to do. She was going to have to tell her friends that she couldn't lie and go to the party and that she'd be going home with her family. She knew that she was risking her reputation among her new friends and especially with Trevor. She feared that he would think she was too immature to continue dating after this, or that his feelings would be hurt.

But regardless of what happened, she couldn't bring herself to blatantly lie to her parents, go to a party that they never would have allowed her to go to, spend time with a boy until very late into the night, and stay the night at a girl's house whose parents were out of town.

Doing those things would destroy all trust that her parents had in her, and she knew it. She would face so much trouble that she wouldn't be able to spend time with Trevor or her new friends anyway, and using such poor judgment would keep her from dating forever, probably.

Decision made, she went to tell Trevor. She found him talking to one of his teammates. They were slapping each other on the back and celebrating a fantastic game. Drew cleared her throat to get their attention.

Trevor turned to see her and said, "Hey, there's my girl." He walked over to her and gave her a little squeeze and a quick kiss on the cheek.

"Great game, Trevor. You did an awesome job out there."

Trevor just beamed with the praise. "You about ready to go? We need to stop and pick up a few things on the way to the party," Trevor said, assuming that she was going.

"Um. . .I need to talk to you about that. I'm not going to be able to go," Drew hesitantly said, biting her lip. "I just can't do it—too many lies and the risk of too much trouble. It's just too much."

Trevor didn't look happy. At first he looked disappointed, but that look quickly turned to anger. "Do you have any idea what you're saying? You're telling me that after a game like this, you're going to leave me dateless and alone at the party of the year? I need you there. You're my girl. You're supposed to be there with me, by my side."

"I can't help it, Trevor. I want to go—really, I do. But I don't want to lie to my parents. And if I were to get caught, we'd never see each other again anyway."

Trevor groaned. "This is what I get for dating a freshman."

"You know, you could be a little more supportive. I'm just trying to do the right thing," Drew tried to explain.

"No, Drew, it's you who could be more supportive." Trevor shook his head in disgust. "So is your mind made up? Is that it? You're not going to go no matter what I say?"

"I'm not going to go." Drew hung her head as she said the words, knowing that she was likely sealing the deal on the end of their relationship.

"Then I guess you'd better go find your

family. It's past your bedtime, and I have to go," Trevor answered sarcastically.

Drew took a deep breath to quell the sob that rose in her throat. She was devastated by his reaction but also miffed that he cared so little about her that he would be angry at her for trying to do the right thing. "Thanks for the support and understanding, Trevor. You've made this all about you, which tells me that you don't really care about me anyway. You only care about how I make you look. I guess I made the right decision. Have fun." With that, she turned and walked away with her head down, hoping he wouldn't see the tears forming in her eyes.

She noticed her parents standing by the car, waiting like they had after the previous game. Trying to compose herself before she got to the car, she stopped and turned to say something to someone passing by. As she did so, she wiped at her eyes and tried to find her smile again. When she turned to face her parents, she looked almost normal. She knew that they could probably see right through her attempts at normalcy but hoped they wouldn't ask about it.

"I changed my mind. I'm going to go with you guys. Is that ice cream offer still good?"

"Of course, dear. It'll be fun. Let's go," Mr. Daniels said with a big grin.

Mrs. Daniels looked hard at Drew, wondering what was bothering her but graciously giving her privacy by not asking.

The girls piled into the backseat, and Mr. Daniels backed the car out of the parking space. Drew could tell that Dani was staring at her, trying to figure out what was going on. She refused to look her in the eye, because Dani would immediately be able to see through her shaky expression of happiness and see that there was sorrow beneath it—and it would probably make Drew cry for real.

As they pulled away from the school, Drew looked out the window and saw Trevor and a bunch of his teammates and some cheerleaders at the end of the parking lot horsing around. It looked like they were getting ready to pack up some cars and head out. They were laughing and having a great time. Trevor sure didn't look sad at all.

Then she saw the unthinkable. Trevor put his arm across the shoulders of one of the varsity cheerleaders. Drew couldn't see who it was exactly, because she was looking at the girl's back, and, in her cheerleading uniform, she looked just like every other cheerleader from the back. Trevor gave her a quick squeeze and started jogging back over to the sports office, presumably to get his things. He sure looked happy, like he didn't have a care in the world. No one would have ever guessed that he was a guy who had supposedly been crushed by a girlfriend he had proclaimed to like so very much that same evening. She felt sorry for the unsuspecting cheerleader who was just happy to have his attention—like Drew had been.

Drew realized that the car was too quiet, and if she didn't do something, they were going to start questioning her. She was in no mood or state of mind to answer questions about the evening. "So, where are we going? We haven't been out for ice cream in forever." She tried to sound energetic and positive.

"I was just wondering about that," Mr. Daniels said. "Should we go somewhere that we can get a burger before we have ice cream? I think everyone is hungry."

"Sounds good to me," Dani spoke up from the backseat.

"Me, too." Drew tried to sound enthusiastic.

After the Danielses were seated and the

waitress took their order for burgers, fries, and chocolate milkshakes all around, Mrs. Daniels looked at Drew and asked, "Okay, what gives? Something happened tonight. You look so sad and disappointed." She waited for Drew to protest that everything was fine, but instead, she could see that Drew was really considering her words carefully.

Finally, Drew realized that she couldn't hold back any longer. She let the tears flow and spilled her emotions and the entire story onto the table. She told her family every detail, even the part about sneaking a ride home with Trevor and the kiss in the bleachers. She spared no detail. Not only was she tired of living what she felt was a lie and being so distant from her family, but she also didn't think it really mattered if she got grounded or into some kind of trouble because she really had nowhere to go now anyway. Plus, it was time for her to get back to being the person she really was deep down.

Finishing the story by recounting the vision of Trevor with his arm around another girl on the way out of the parking lot that night, Drew dried her eyes with resolve not to cry over him anymore. He didn't care about her needs and wants and was willing to pressure her to do things that made her very uncomfortable. Drew knew that she was better off without him, but dreams die hard, and her mom knew that.

Just as Drew was finishing her story, the waitress brought the food. Drew dived into her burger with a vengeance, feeding her body and nursing her broken heart. Everyone at the table took a few moments to begin to eat and also to let Drew's words sink in.

Dani remained quiet, afraid to break the moment and wanting Drew to continue to come to her new realizations. She was so very happy that Drew had made the right decision, and it really sounded like she had grown through the experience. She hoped that her parents wouldn't be too hard on her.

"Drew. . .there are a lot of things I'd like to say. Are you ready for me to respond, or do you need more time?" Mrs. Daniels asked.

"Go ahead, Mom. But I pretty much already know what you're going to say."

"Oh? Try me. What am I about to say?"

"You're going to tell me how mad you are at me about the after-game thing last week. You're going to tell me that I'm way too young to have a boyfriend, and that I proved it by not telling you all about it. You're going to tell me that I shouldn't have kissed him. I'm going to be punished for sneaking around and for doing things that I knew you wouldn't approve of like the makeup and the clothes. Basically, you're going to tell me how disappointed you are in me. Right?"

"Well, sweetie, I'm speaking for myself, and your dad may feel much differently, but that is about the exact opposite of what I want to say to you."

"Huh? What do you mean?"

"I have never, ever been more proud of you, Drew. You faced some very grown-up things in a few short weeks. And you were tempted by the glitter and sparkle of adult life and you made some decisions that I wouldn't have approved of, that's for sure. But Drew, look at the result. You have surprised me by the fact that when push came to shove, you gave up all of the things that you wanted so badly and chose what was right. You lost a lot tonight, by your own choice. But by doing that, you gained even more."

"I think that your mom is trying to say that you've grown through this," Mr. Daniels explained. "And you've shown us clearly what type of young lady you really are. We really like what we see."

Drew was in tears again—this time, tears of relief. She was so blown away by her parents' reaction that she didn't know what to say. She thought of Pastor Michaels's words. "Remember last week when Pastor Michaels talked about how when we impose our own will over God's plan, that it's like saying, 'I've got everything under control'? And that is a pride issue. . .you know. . .to think that we know more than God." At her parents' nod, she continued. "Well, I said those words several times this week: 'I've got it all under control.' Turns out, I didn't. Pastor Michaels was right. And you guys, my parents, kind of act as a stand-in for God. So, your rules—or what you want for me and from me—are just an extension of God's will. Right?"

Flabbergasted by the maturity of her realization, Mr. and Mrs. Daniels both said, "You're very right."

"Well, I guess what I want is to live for God and walk according to His will. That means I don't have everything under control. . .you guys do. I'm not saying I'll be perfect, but I guess I just want something different—I want to do it right. Does that make sense?"

"Perfect sense."

"For the record," Dani jumped in, "I totally agree with you, Drew. And I'm so glad to hear you saying this. I was really getting worried about you. I guess I should have known that, as smart as you are, you'd come around."

"Thanks, sis. Can you ever forgive me for the way I've treated you this past month?"

"Of course I can. I love you. . .it's forgiven. Now, let's just move on. I'd like us to commit to supporting each other in doing the right thing from now on. I feel like I should have tried a lot harder to keep you on the straight and narrow. I guess I was too hurt and bitter. I'm sorry for that."

"Dani, you have nothing to be sorry for. You're the best sister a girl could ever hope for. And I love you, too."

"Drew, one thing you may not have thought of yet," Mrs. Daniels mentioned, "and we can talk more about this throughout the weekend, but it's going to be tough to go back to school on Monday. We need to have a plan for you and also to surround you in prayer that you'll be able to stand your ground no matter what."

"Great point, Mom. Monday seems so far away right now, though. This is what I care most about." She spread her hands to gesture to her family at the table. She was home.

Chapter 12

REAL FRIENDS

After staying in and laying low on Sunday, except for attending church, Drew felt mentally and emotionally prepared for school. Dani was so good to encourage her and promise support. Really, though, Drew had done nothing wrong, and people broke up all the time. She hoped her new friends wouldn't abandon her, too. She was realistic enough to know that Trevor was their golden boy, so it would be up to him and what he said about her that would determine how everyone else responded to her. Her best bet, she knew, was to look confident and happy when she went to school. Hanging her head and hiding from the group would only fuel the impression of her immaturity.

She rose early and carefully dressed for school. Wanting to look great, but not like she was trying too hard, Drew selected her favorite pair of jeans and one of the new tops that she bought for herself. It was important to keep being herself. She did promise her mom that she wouldn't sneak makeup anymore, though. As part of that deal, her parents had agreed to a few new things that she was allowed to wear. She could now wear light lipstick or colored lip gloss, soft blush on her cheeks, and mascara to lengthen her eyelashes. Still forbidden were any colors of eye shadow, eyeliner, or lip liner. Mrs. Daniels felt that those things were way too "made up" for a freshman and took away from the girls' natural beauty. So Drew carefully applied her makeup within the new guidelines—no more sneaking. One last look in the mirror reflected success. She really had to admit that the look was much softer and prettier than the garish effect of lots of makeup. Her mom had been right about that one.

Threading her favorite belt through the frayed loops on her jeans and securing the buckle as she went downstairs to the kitchen, Drew realized that her stomach was too upset to eat.

Her mom must have known that she'd feel that way, because all that she handed to Drew when she arrived in the kitchen was a piece of buttered toast. Drew, grateful that it was only toast, took the plate and sat down to eat.

The time passed quickly, and there were no more reasons to stall. Drew and Dani got ready to catch the bus in front of their house. Taking a shuddering deep breath, Drew grabbed her things and prepared to leave the house.

With her hand on the door, Mrs. Daniels asked if she could pray for her.

"Of course, Mom. Thanks."

"Father, please be with Drew today. Give her peace and wisdom as she faces this difficult situation. Let her find favor with the students whom You have selected to be her friends, and let her peacefully accept that some will not turn out to be true friends. Help her be strong and stand for You. Keep both of my girls safe at school today and make them strong and powerful examples of You and Your love. Amen."

"Thanks, Mom." Drew hugged her mom and started to leave.

"I love you both."

"We love you too, Mom," Drew and Dani answered simultaneously.

Arriving at school, Drew took a deep breath as the bus squealed to a stop. Dani reached over and took her sister's hand. "It's going to be okay. The first hour is the hardest. After that, it just gets easier. I promise."

"You're the best, Dani. I am so glad you're my sister and my best friend." She took another deep breath, fluffed her hair, squared her shoulders, and went down the steps of the bus. "Here we go."

The girls walked into the school with their heads held high. They talked and laughed and acted as though they didn't have a care in the world. They made it all the way to their lockers without bumping into anyone upsetting to Drew. Students still gave her the usual comments about her clothes and the halls were peppered with the usual shouts of "Hi, Drew" all along the way. She hadn't lost her status yet. But Drew wondered if that was just because news hadn't traveled that fast.

"You're here? I can't believe you're okay." Cara, their longtime friend, came running up to the girls.

"Yeah, I guess you heard, huh? Well, there was no way that my mom was going to let me skip school just because I was sad about breaking up with Trevor."

"Breaking up with Trevor? That's not what I'm talking about at all. Didn't you hear what happened?" Cara was breathless with excitement.

"I guess I haven't heard. What happened?" Drew asked Cara just to be polite but wasn't really interested in anyone else's gossip; she had enough of her own to deal with.

"Well. . ." Cara excitedly started her story. "I guess there was a big party at Samantha's house after the game. Anyway, there was drinking, some drugs, and loud music. Neighbors called the cops, and a bunch of kids got arrested for the alcohol, drugs, and for disturbing the peace. Sam's older sister also got in trouble for providing alcohol to minors. I guess some of the guys from school even had fake IDs. It's a big mess."

"Oh my goodness, I can't believe it. I was supposed to be at that party. I chose not to go because I didn't want to lie to my parents, and that's why Trevor dumped me."

"What a jerk! Well, he got what was coming to him."

"No, I don't wish that kind of trouble on anyone. I feel really bad that they all went through that this weekend. I had no idea. Here I was all wrapped up in my own little drama, which was nothing in comparison. I wonder if they'll be at school."

"I saw Sam already but not Trevor, and I don't know who else got into trouble. I'm sure we'll find out more as the day goes on. But I'm really sorry, Drew. I'm sure you must have been really hurt."

"Yeah, it's been a tough weekend. But Dani and I have had a chance to spend a lot of time together, and I've missed that. So something good came of it all."

"Hang in there today, Drew. Your real friends will show what they're made of. The rest don't really matter anyway." Cara and Dani shared a first-period class, so they left together after making sure that Drew would be okay.

Drew finished putting her books in her locker and then turned to go to class. As she turned, she bumped into Samantha. Sam's eyes looked haunted and scared. Drew immediately realized that the weekend had taken a big toll on her. Sam looked at Drew in disgust and walked the other way. Drew saw that Sam's reaction really had nothing to do with her. She was just taking out her own fears on whoever was near. It meant nothing, and Drew decided not to let it bother her. One down, one more to go. Trevor was the only other one she was nervous about seeing. The rest would work itself out.

Morning classes passed by too quickly, and it was time for the dreaded lunch hour. Part of her felt that it would be best to go to Trevor's table and just sit down to have lunch there. She hadn't actually been uninvited. But she didn't want to suffer the humiliation of being publicly shunned. Or, on the off chance that he was happy to see her, Drew didn't want to send the message that his treatment of her was okay. So her plan was to sit with Dani, Cara, and their other friends at lunch. Drew even brought her lunch to school that day so that she wouldn't have to walk past Trevor and his friends to get a hot lunch.

Sliding into a seat at the end of the table, Drew kept her back to Trevor's table. She realized that she hadn't seen him all day, though.

Suddenly she wondered if he were even at school that day. Ah, there he was. Across the lunchroom, she saw his broad shoulders towering above the other students. Sadly, she slumped into her seat and made sure not to look back. She needed a few moments to regain her resolve.

The girls chatted their way through lunch with all sorts of small talk. Drew contributed a lot of grunts and groans. Finally she realized what a drag she had been and apologized. "I'm really sorry for being in such a slump. I guess this is harder than I thought it would be."

"It's totally understandable—" Cara started to say but stopped short.

Samantha approached the table and wanted to talk to Drew. The other girls scooted down a little bit to make room for Sam, but they weren't about to leave Drew alone with her yet.

"So, Drew, did you have fun on Friday night? Did you get to go home with Mommy and Daddy and get a special treat for being such a good girl?"

"What's your problem, Sam?" Drew straightened her back, not willing to let Sam's anger get to her. "Didn't you have a curfew or rules when you were in the ninth grade? Eh, maybe you didn't. Maybe your parents let you do whatever you wanted. I guess that didn't pay off too well for you, according to rumors. Looks like I made the right choice. Sure wish you guys could support that."

"Support that? You want me to support your abandonment and betrayal of us, your supposed friends?" Sam was truly shocked at the suggestion, and it just made Drew realize that they weren't operating with the same moral compass.

"Yes, I do think you should have supported me—if you were truly my friend, that is. A true friend wouldn't want to put her friend in a situation that was uncomfortable. A true friend would back up the tough decisions and allow for the differences between us. A false friend only wants what she wants for herself and has no thought for others."

"Are you suggesting that I fit your description of a false friend?" Sam was getting angry.

"Well, Sam, think about it. It's all I know of you. During our short friendship, everything was great as long as I was going along with what you guys wanted. As soon as I took a stand as an individual person, you took it personally and got angry with me, even to the point of dropping me as your friend. I don't really want to discuss it any further. I can't convince you, and I don't have to. Just think about what I said. I have to get to class."

Chapter 13

LESSONS, THE HARD WAY

As the week went on, Drew learned more details about last Friday night. The gang all showed up at Sam's house after the game. Her parents were out of town, so the closest thing to an adult was her twenty-two-year-old sister. They started a bonfire in the fire pit, and Sam's sister went to buy them a bunch of beer. Apparently Trevor even used a fake ID to buy beer, too. Sam, Trevor, and the rest of them stood around the bonfire, drinking beer for hours. Eventually, things got a little crazy. Someone brought out some drugs to pass around, and most of them sampled it. Kids were splashing in the pool and screaming at all hours. Finally, at about one in the morning, one of the neighbors apparently had enough with the noise and constant commotion—maybe they even suspected the kids had drugs—and called the police.

Three police cars arrived with lights and sirens blaring. They pulled into the driveway sideways to block in all of the cars. They went around to the backyard immediately, called a stop to the party, and herded all of the students onto the back porch. Several were let go when it was determined that they hadn't been drinking. Most of the others were told to walk in a straight line and touch their fingers to their noses. Some were too drunk to even be tested. All of those who were detained were eventually read their rights and placed in a squad car to be taken to the police station.

The majority of the teens were charged with the consumption of alcohol as a minor. Drew was told that a charge like that would mean a fine and some community service, most likely. Many of them, including Sam and Trevor, were charged with that plus a charge related to the drug use; and Trevor even got in trouble for buying alcohol with a fake ID. It sounded like Trevor was in a lot of trouble. Kids were even talking about him being sent away somewhere. And a couple of others, including Sam's sister, were charged as adults with crimes related to supplying alcohol to minors. All of them were taken to the police station, formally charged, fingerprinted, and locked up until their parents could be reached. They each had to call their parents to come and pick them up from the police station—what a tough call that must have been. Sam and her sister actually had to stay in jail overnight until their parents could get back into town to pick them up.

It was a horrible mess, and it broke Drew's heart that her friends—real friends or not—had to go through something like that. Even though things turned out badly with Trevor, Drew still cared about him and would never want to see him hurting like this. She couldn't even imagine how he must have felt there in the police station while waiting for his parents to arrive. And she had no idea what the legal situation would be. She hoped that, no matter what happened, this would be something that the Lord would use to wake him up.

It was a strange week, because Drew knew they were ignoring her. She supposed that being ignored was better than being ridiculed or called out for her decisions. By Thursday, Drew had basically let go and realized that they weren't going to come around. So she just stuck with her sister and her real friends and enjoyed her cheerleading squad. She really had no need for those older kids, anyway. She had a lot more in common with the others.

On Thursday, just as they were finishing up their lunches, Dani said, "Um, Drew. . . Trevor's on his way over here. Be strong."

Drew panicked for a minute. She wasn't prepared to talk to him, because she didn't know what he was going to say to her. She could handle being ignored, but to be confronted by Trevor would be very difficult for her. She said a quick prayer for peace and wisdom and hoped that she'd be strong.

"Hey, Drew. Mind if I sit down for a minute?" Trevor asked when he got to the table.

The other girls took the cue and left the table, giving them a moment alone. As she squeezed past her sister, Dani gave Drew's shoulder a little squeeze for strength.

"Sure, it's a free country." Drew motioned to an empty seat, not quite being rude, but not being too gracious, either.

Trevor was quiet for a minute. It was clear that he was uncomfortable and didn't quite know how to start. "First, I just wanted to apologize for how I acted. I never should have pressured you like I did, and I feel horrible for being such a jerk."

"Thank you for saying that. I appreciate it." Drew wasn't about to gush or make it easy for him, but she had no reason to make it any more difficult than it already was.

"You must have really felt bad after the way I treated you."

Drew nodded and wiped at a tear that she had tried unsuccessfully to will away.

"The thing is, I don't know what came over me. It's not like me to be so insensitive."

"Power." Drew barely whispered the one word that came to her mind.

"Did you say 'power'? What do you mean?"

"I mean that the power got to you. You were having a pretty exciting few weeks; and the power of getting exactly what you wanted was getting to you, and you demanded your way from everyone, even from me."

Trevor thought for a moment. "I guess you're right. Anyway, I'm sorry. You did the right thing. . . . Well. . .obviously, by the way things turned out, you did the right thing."

"Thank you. I know I did. It was difficult, though."

"I'm sure it was. You're much stronger than I am." Trevor hung his head, overcome with regret and sadness. "Is there anything I can do to patch things up between us? I'd really like to keep seeing you, Drew."

"Trevor, I like you, I really do. But I think I've learned that there are big differences between kids our ages, and I'm just not ready to make that leap. I want to enjoy the place I am right now and not rush things. Plus, my personal opinion is that you need some time to focus on what you want for yourself. I don't want to be a distraction in that process. You have a lot on your plate, a lot that you're facing. I think you should face first things first—and not worry about a girlfriend right now. Trevor, maybe it's time you stop sleeping in on Sunday mornings and start going to church. That's where you'll find the answers you're looking for."

"I'll think about it. And I understand. I'm

not giving up, though. Maybe in a few months, when all of this is behind us, maybe you'll want to give it another try then."

"We never know what the future may hold; but at this point, I have no plans to get involved with someone this year. I've learned my lesson."

"Well, then, good for you. I hope I've learned some lessons, too."

"Me, too, Trevor. Me, too."

"Can we still be friends?" Trevor asked hopefully.

"Of course we can be friends. But I'm sticking with my best friends for the most part. I'll see you around, and we can be nice to each other; but I don't see us hanging out like we once did. It's okay, though. It's part of the process. You see, I made some mistakes in all of this, too. I was a really bad friend and sister during my supposed climb to the top, and I won't be letting that happen again. I'm sure you can understand."

"I've learned a lot from you, Drew. I hope you find all of the happiness you deserve."

They parted for class. Drew felt strong and incredibly relieved. God answered her prayers and gave her strength she didn't think she had—and also gave her a way out when there seemed to be no way. As she walked to class, she quietly thanked Him for being with her and giving her the words to say. She also prayed for Trevor and the difficult situation he was in legally. She prayed for mercy for him and that he would learn about life and love through this situation. She then thanked the Lord for guiding her through the tough choices she had faced and asked Him to keep leading her every step of the way. For the first time that week, she felt happy. She walked to class with her head held high and with a smile on her face, confident that God had everything under control.

The next three chapters tell the story of what happened to Drew when she decided to give in to the pressure by doing what her friends were asking her to do.

Chapter 11

PARTY TIME!

"I'm definitely going to go. You're sure it's okay to spend the night at Sam's?"

"Oh, yeah. She told me it was fine," Trevor assured Drew.

"All right, then I'm going to go tell my parents. I'll be right back." Drew ran off to find her family waiting patiently by the car.

"So, what's your plan, Drew?" Mrs. Daniels asked when Drew ran up. "By the way," she threw in before Drew could answer about her plans, "you looked fantastic out there again. You do such a great job." Mr. Daniels and Dani agreed.

"Thanks, guys. I'm so glad you came."

Drew was happy to hear their comments but still nervous, because she knew she was about to lie to them. "Well, about tonight, I'd like to go with the squad to eat and then with the other girls over to Sam's house to spend the night. I have clothes and stuff already in my gym bag from earlier today. And I'll just have someone drop me off sometime in the morning." She left out the fact that it wouldn't be just girls at Sam's and that Sam's parents were out of town.

"That sounds fine. Her parents will be home, right?"

"Of course, Mom. Do you want the number?"

"Well, let me have the number in case of an emergency, but I trust you."

Drew gave her Sam's phone number, kissed her parents, said good-bye to Dani, who had been strangely quiet, and ran off to join her friends. When she got to Trevor's side, she said, "It's all set. I do need to tell Sam to make sure her sister knows that my mom might call. She probably won't, but just in case something happens, I want her to be prepared."

"I already told her all about that. So it's all set?" Trevor flashed a huge grin. "Excellent. Let's go. We have to stop at the store on the way." He opened the passenger door for her and, like a perfect gentleman, helped her fasten her seat belt.

"Why don't you wait here?" Trevor suggested when they arrived at the grocery store.

"Okay, if you want me to." Drew found that odd but figured he was just in a big hurry to get to the party.

Drew sat in the car, looking through Trevor's CDs for about fifteen minutes. She was just about to get out of the car to go look for him when she saw him pushing a full cart toward the car. He went straight to the trunk and loaded it up, got in the car, and they left for the party. It was about a fifteen-minute drive to Sam's house, but it flew by, because Trevor held Drew's hand the whole way there.

When they arrived at the party, the bonfire was already blazing and people were milling around Samantha's big backyard. A few people were swimming, even though it was a bit chilly. Drew surveyed the yard and saw at least fifty people there already, but many were clearly not in high school anymore as evidenced by the beer cans they were holding.

Sam came running up to Trevor and Drew. "Hey, guys. Glad you're here." Turning her attention to Trevor, she asked, "Did you get it?"

He answered, "Yep. It's in the trunk. I'll unload it in a few minutes."

"Oh, it's okay. I'll help you. We can get it now," Drew offered.

Laughing, Trevor said, "Okay, you asked for it." He popped the trunk open with the remote on his key ring and they walked around to the back.

Drew gasped when she saw the contents of the trunk. There were two or three bags full of chips and snacks right next to three cases of beer.

"How did you buy that?" Drew was shocked and afraid when she realized what kind of party this was going to be.

"It's called a fake ID, my dear." Trevor laughed. "Welcome to high school and the party of the year. Grab a bag and let's go."

Drew grabbed the bags of chips; she wasn't sure that she wanted anything to do with the beer. Walking into the house with the food,

Drew was shocked to see kids she knew from school smoking cigarettes and drinking. She had heard about parties like this but had no idea this kind of thing actually went on in her school.

Trevor immediately popped the top off of a beer and took a big drink, as did Samantha. Drew just stared at them for a second. It surprised her that they could drink the beer so fast; it meant that this probably wasn't the first time. They offered her a beer and she declined. It was too much for her, but they laughed.

Samantha said, "If you want to run with the big kids, you need to act like one." They both continued to laugh but didn't pressure her anymore.

Trevor and Drew walked through the party—Drew with her can of soda and Trevor with his beer—stopping to talk to little groups of kids. Eventually they all wound up out by the fire. Cans of beer were tossed around, making sure that no one was left empty-handed. Spirits were high; the party was in full swing.

Drew asked Trevor what time it was and how long he would be able to stay. "I'm just concerned about you driving home after drinking," she explained.

"Oh, don't worry about that, sweet thing." Trevor grinned and put his arm around her. "I'm not going anywhere tonight. I wouldn't leave you alone in this strange place. What kind of boyfriend would I be if I did that?"

Drew was so torn. She was happy to be there. It made her feel so mature and part of the in crowd. But to get there that night, she had told no fewer than three big lies. She had broken some very important rules. She was sleeping over at a house where there were no adults. The sleepover was turning out to be boys and girls, including her boyfriend. She was also being offered alcohol and hanging out with kids who were drinking. Her own boyfriend even used a fake ID to buy beer. Even the fact that he was her "boyfriend" would have upset her parents.

As she attempted to sort through some of those truths, she started to smell something funny. It was like nothing she had ever smelled before, and she was pretty sure she didn't want to know what it was. She looked around the circle and saw kids smoking stuff that didn't look like regular cigarettes. Drugs! Someone had brought drugs to the party.

Drew stood and contemplated her situation for a few moments. She could go home.

But if she called home, she would be in big trouble. Perhaps her best bet was to hope that nothing happened and that she didn't get caught. Tomorrow, it would all be over and she could go back to normal life, she hoped. But since she was there and had decided not to leave, and since she had decided not to let herself get in this predicament again, she thought it might be a good idea to take her opportunity to try some things that she may not have a chance to do again.

So in the next hour, she took a few puffs of Trevor's cigarette; she drank a beer, plus a few sips of a different kind of drink that Trevor had; and, with her judgment even more skewed by the alcohol, she actually allowed herself to be convinced to try the drugs that were being passed around.

She really didn't like how she was starting to feel—kind of fuzzy and like she was in slow motion—but after a while she started to get used to it and went for more beer. She really didn't want to get out of control, but she did want to have fun. So this is what it meant to party? It felt great to Drew. . .like second nature. She looked at her watch and was shocked to see that it was one in the morning. The time was going so fast, and Drew didn't want the night to end.

Trevor came up behind her, put his arms around her, and squeezed. "How's my girl doing? You having a good time?"

"Mmm-hmm," Drew murmured as she settled the back of her head against his broad chest. She liked the way it felt to be held, and for a minute she forgot where she was. He turned her around to face him and leaned in for a kiss. It was a much softer and longer kiss than the one they shared in the bleachers. It felt much more grown-up, and in no way did it make her giggle. Drew hoped that the moment would never stop.

Trevor pulled away slightly and said, "I like kissing you."

"Mmm, I like to be kissed." She smiled and kissed him again.

"Here," Trevor said as the drugs came around through the group and back to them. He offered her some. She tried to decline, but Trevor teased her a bit and convinced her to have some more. "You can't really know how you'll feel until you try it for real. That one hit you took earlier just isn't enough to get the full effect."

Drew took it out of his hands and put it to

her lips and lightly inhaled.

"Oh, no, that's not how you do it. Watch." Trevor demonstrated for her and then put it to her lips once more.

As Drew inhaled, she wondered why he wanted her to smoke it so badly. She let the thought pass, though, and began to really feel the effects.

Trevor leaned in for another kiss, and this time, neither of them pulled away. Drew became a bit afraid that she'd never want this to stop, so she pulled away. "Let's go inside and get a snack. I'm starving."

"Okay, but you're not getting off that easily. We'll pick that up again a little later, maybe when we're alone."

Drew was afraid to consider what that might mean. But it didn't matter yet. The party was in full swing and some people were still arriving. She reminded herself that she was a smart girl and that she had everything under control.

Chapter 12

JUST NOT RIGHT

Back at home, Mr. and Mrs. Daniels tried to relax and watch some TV before bed. But something was just not sitting right with them. They were uneasy about some of the things that Drew had said and some of the signals they read from her, but they had a difficult time deciding what it was that made them so uneasy.

"She was nervous," Mrs. Daniels said. "She was nervous and fidgety when she was talking to us. Do you think that's what is bugging us?"

"That could be it. You know, I've been thinking. . ." Mr. Daniels hesitated. "I don't want to ask Dani to betray Drew, but maybe she knows something."

"We could talk to her. Or I could always try calling Samantha's mom."

"That's a good idea. Do that first, and then, if we still need to, we can talk to Dani."

Mrs. Daniels dialed the phone and waited for someone to pick up. Finally someone answered, but the background noise was so loud that she could barely hear the person on the other end of the line.

Casting a nervous glance at her husband, Mrs. Daniels said, "I'm looking for Samantha's mom. Is she available?"

"No, lady, she's out of town," the boy slurred and then hung up.

Mrs. Daniels sat and stared at the phone in her hand like it was a snake. After recounting the brief conversation to her husband, they were both so concerned that Mr. Daniels immediately went upstairs to wake Dani up and ask her to join them in the family room.

Dani came down the stairs, sleepily rubbing her eyes. When she realized what they were asking her, she struggled over what to tell her parents. She wasn't willing to lie, but she really wanted to protect her sister as much as she could.

"Danielle,"—it was never a good thing when Dad used her full name—"if you know anything about where your sister is and what she might be doing, we need to know. It seems as though there is a lot more to the story than we were told, and we're concerned that she could be getting into some trouble. This is definitely not the time to try to protect your sister from getting caught. She could be facing much greater dangers than that."

Dani realized that this situation was much bigger than just wanting to protect her sister. Her love for Drew meant that she needed to help her parents help her sister. She wound up telling them everything she knew, starting with the first time Drew got a ride home from Trevor, and about the kiss in the bleachers, to what she had heard about this party around school. She told them that there was no adult there and that there was to be alcohol and possibly even drugs. She also let them know what she had been hearing about Trevor and how he mistreated girls.

Her parents were horrified, but they set their horror aside for a moment and sprang into action. They looked up Samantha's address and took off for the house, afraid of what they might find when they got there. Dani stayed at home and went up to her room after they left so she could think and pray about the situation. She was glad that everything was finally coming to light, because she had been so worried about Drew. But she was also worried that Drew would never forgive her for telling their parents what had been going on. Dani knew that now more than ever before, her sister needed her prayers and her support.

Bonfire blazing, people laughing and milling around the yard, Drew and Trevor were having a great time being silly and raucous by the fire. One thing Drew noticed about alcohol was that it made her less inhibited. Things that would have made her uncomfortable just a few hours before suddenly became completely acceptable and desirable. She became very comfortable with Trevor's touches and even initiated some herself, which made him very happy.

After an hour or so of flirting around the fire, Trevor wanted Drew to come with him to find a private place for a few minutes. She knew that it would mean more kissing; and even though she was scared, she really wanted to go. They decided that the pool shed would be a great place for them to hang out. On their way to the pool shed, Drew heard something funny coming from the front of the house. Wondering what was happening, she pulled Trevor toward the front, even though he was trying to pull her toward the shed.

When she got a little closer, she heard shouting. "Where is my daughter? Someone better bring me to her *now*!"

Drew instantly recognized her father's voice and turned to Trevor, hoping he could help her make sense of it all. Her mind was fuzzy because of the alcohol and drugs, so she couldn't fully grasp what was happening to her—and she even started giggling.

Trevor shot her a look and said, "This really isn't funny."

"Everything's funny." Drew giggled again. She was completely incapable of grasping the gravity of the situation. "I know what I'll do. I'm going in to the bathroom so I can clean myself up before I see them." She ran off through the back entrance to find the bathroom before her parents found her.

In the bright yellow bathroom, Drew took a look in the mirror over the sink. She was horrified by what she saw. Her clothes were a mess, her makeup was smeared, and she knew that she reeked of smoke—cigarette and bonfire smoke. As soon as she thought of the smoking, her stomach began to turn. The combination of beer and smoke on an empty stomach were quickly becoming too much for her to handle. As the bubbling continued to rise in her belly, she turned and lunged for the toilet where she became sick, emptying the contents of her stomach. Feeling a bit better, she washed her face and hands and tried to straighten her hair. Wishing she could stall a little longer, she knew that her time was up. It was time to face the music.

She slowly opened the door a crack. She had no idea what she would say to her mom and dad. She realized that she had disappointed them in just about every possible way in that one night. As she was coming to her senses and remembering everything about the night and what led up to it, Drew wished with all her heart that she could go back and have another chance to do things the right way. But it was too late.

She saw her parents enter the house and approach Sam's sister, who pointed toward the bathroom. They both saw her at the same time, and there was a moment of eye contact that Drew would never forget. Her mom was crying and wiping her eyes. She looked so sad. Her dad mostly looked mad. Drew wasn't sure which one she was dreading the most: the disappointment or the anger.

Drew started to open her mouth to speak, but Dad cut her off and said, "I'm not interested in hearing anything from you right now, Drew. Just collect your things and let's go."

Mrs. Daniels covered her mouth with her tissue and sobbed harder when she heard her husband's words.

Drew quietly got her jacket from the hook on the back of the door. She started the long, shameful walk out to the car and couldn't lift her head to look her parents in the eye. They said nothing.

She sat in the backseat, silent, alone, listening to her mom crying softly in the front seat. Suddenly her words came back to her, haunting her: *"I've got everything under control."* She regretted those words so much. But it was too late. She had failed.

Mr. Daniels started to walk back into the house to talk to Samantha but decided he would be better off taking his daughter home and coming back. As her dad walked to his car door, Drew caught a glimpse of Trevor standing on the side of the house, watching the scene unfold. He shook his head in disgust; he looked angry. For a brief moment, Drew felt a bit of shock to realize that he was angry with her instead of being worried about her. She shrugged off those feelings, because she had much more important things to deal with.

Her dad got into the car, backed out of the driveway, and headed down the street. Before they got to the end of the block, they heard sirens and saw lights flashing. Three police cars screamed past them and pulled into the driveway they had just left. Policemen got out of the car with their hands on their guns and started shouting at people in the yard.

Mr. Daniels continued driving away, but they all realized immediately what could have happened if they had arrived five minutes later than they had. That realization dissolved Drew into tears. She knew she deserved to be there facing the police with her "friends," but she was so glad that she wasn't.

A few minutes later, at home, the

Danielses all walked into the house; and Drew, feeling sick again, ran to the bathroom. After she was sick for the second time, she decided to take a quick shower to attempt to rid herself of the filth that covered her from the evening. She stood in the shower, under the hot water for a long time. It was difficult to hurry, because the room seemed to be swaying. She finally finished and got dressed.

"Mom. . .Dad. . ." She didn't know what to say to them when she entered the family room. They were sitting silently in the dimly lit room, not even speaking to each other.

"Drew, I honestly don't know if we have it in us to talk to you about this tonight." Mr. Daniels had his head in his hands and he wouldn't look at her. Drew's mom stared blankly at her, almost as though she didn't even know her. Perhaps she felt that she didn't.

"Please. . .I need to. . .I can't leave it until tomorrow. . .we need to fix this." Drew begged for their attention, because the thought of having to wait until tomorrow to face them was too much for her.

"Drew, there is no quick fix for this. And it really doesn't matter what you need right now.

Your mom and I just don't have it in us to figure out what we want to say or need to say to you. It's going to take time. And you're just going to have to deal with that."

Drew hung her head in sadness and embarrassment, knowing that she had really crushed her parents and destroyed their trust in her. She would do anything for the chance to take back her actions that evening. But that wasn't going to happen. The only thing for her to do was to go to bed.

"I'm so sorry. I love you both. Good night."

"We love you, too, Drew. Good night."

Climbing into her bed, Drew was careful not to wake Dani, who was in her own bed across the room, pretending to be asleep. Dani lay there, afraid that Drew would be mad at her for all she had told their parents, so she didn't let on that she was awake.

Drew lay in bed for a long time as tears quietly soaked her pillow. So much had died that night. It was the death of her innocence in many ways. It was the death of her parents' trust in her. It was the death of her faith in people. It was the death of her faith in herself. She knew that somehow she would have to find a way to resurrect her faith in God before any of those things could be restored.

Chapter 13

TRUTH AND CONSEQUENCES

Drew woke up slowly the morning after the party. She rolled over and noticed that she was still nauseated and forgot, for a moment, why she felt sick. Suddenly, memories from the night before started coming back to her. With a loud groan, she turned over and covered her head with her pillow, trying to escape the memories, even for just one more moment.

After narrowly escaping a run-in with the police, Drew felt equal amounts of regret and relief. She was so regretful about the things she had done, and she knew there were consequences for them that she still had to face. But she was also so very relieved that she escaped a legal problem. Also, as difficult as it was for her to admit to herself, she was relieved that she had been found out. It was too stressful to carry on like she had been. It was just not natural for her to lie to her parents; and, looking back on the night before, she didn't like the person she had been. Plus, she knew that she had really been in over her head and was headed for some real trouble. Who knew what last night would have led to after alcohol and drugs. . .she could have done anything. And it was beginning to seem like Trevor knew that and had been happily taking advantage of it.

Drew sat up in bed and looked over at her sister. Dani was lying on her side with her eyes open, looking back at Drew.

"I'm so sorry," Dani whispered.

"Why are you sorry?" Drew was confused.

"I totally ratted you out. I told them everything I knew and everything I suspected. I'd just had enough with worrying about you all on my own, and I thought I was doing the right thing."

"You did do the right thing, and you have nothing to be sorry for."

"Drew, what happened last night? Were

there really drugs and alcohol at that party? You didn't do any, did you? Please tell me you didn't." Dani had so many questions for Drew.

"I wish I could tell you that I did nothing wrong, but I can't. Everything you heard about the party was true. I wish I could say that I was strong and didn't do any of it, but I'm so embarrassed to admit, I did it all."

"Drew! Seriously? Why? I'm so bummed. I mean. . .I just wish this hadn't happened at all. I should have stopped it somehow. What did Mom and Dad say?"

"Slow down, sis. It's not your fault, and there was nothing you could have done to stop it. It was my choice and my fault. And believe me, I wish it hadn't happened, too. As for Mom and Dad, we haven't even talked about it yet. I guess it's about time for me to go face the music. Stalling isn't going to help things a bit."

Drew got out of bed, leaving Dani to think over all she had just heard. She brushed her teeth and washed her face, stopping to look at herself for a minute. As she stared at her reflection, she just couldn't figure out how things had gotten so far out of hand. She tied her hair back into a ponytail and went downstairs. Her mom was in the kitchen, making coffee, and her dad was sitting at the table. The night's sleep and the fresh light of day seemed to have calmed them a bit, so she took a seat with her dad and waited for someone to say something. No one did.

"Mom, Dad, I can't tell you how sorry I am. I really screwed up. But I can honestly tell you that I'm relieved to have it over. It was really getting out of hand, and I felt kind of trapped. . . you know, in over my head."

"Oh, Drew. Where did we go wrong? What should we have done differently to teach you better about right and wrong? We thought we were doing all the right things," Mrs. Daniels said, crying.

"Mom, you have done a fantastic job. Look at Dani. I'm just different. I'm more stubborn; and I guess I have to learn from my own mistakes, which is part of being stubborn—but it's not your fault. I have learned so much from all of this. I mean, I know that I'll be punished, but believe me, there is no punishment that could be worse than how I feel already. I never knew what real regret felt like. I know I've hurt you. . .that just kills me."

"Oh, Drew, this is so far beyond

punishment." Mr. Daniels fingered the corner of his unread newspaper. "Yes, there will be consequences, but it's more than that. We need to change the way we do things around here. You've lost our trust, and it's going to take a long time to earn that back. And," Mr. Daniels continued, "just so you understand, it's not that we want to withhold our trust as a punishment, it's just that we can't let go of you right now for fear of what you'll do to yourself. We're going to have to keep you really close for a long time."

"I understand, Dad. I don't blame you. Whatever you want or need from me, whatever I can do, I will do gladly. I am just so grateful to have been spared what a lot of my friends probably faced last night, and I'm so relieved to have been saved from myself and from what I might have done."

"Drew, you're going to need to step down from cheerleading," her mom said without looking at her.

Tears sprang to Drew's eyes. "Oh, Mom, I was so afraid you'd say that. Is that really necessary? I mean, it's a school-sponsored activity. . . wait. . .you're right. I just got finished saying that I would do whatever it took. If you think it's important, I won't question you."

Mr. Daniels sat up in his chair. "Now, Drew, that tells me that you are serious in your remorse. Thank you for that. But yes, it's important. For one thing, we don't want you associating with those kids anymore. For another thing, we feel that you need to get your focus off of yourself, your looks, and the attention and all that comes with cheerleading and get back to basics like school and good friends."

"Okay, Dad. I can understand that."

"As for the rest of your punishment, it's just that things are going to change. No more staying out with friends. No sleepovers, no trips to the mall. You're going to go to school and come home. You and your sister can find your relationship again. You can go to church and youth group activities. But that's about it." Mr. Daniels held up his hand. "Before you ask, I don't know how long. I guess until we feel you are safe from yourself and your poor decisions."

Drew sat with her head down. It was difficult to look her parents in the eye, so she just took in their words.

"Drew, your dad and I really want to encourage you to get some counseling from one of the pastors at church. We'd like to see you get back to your roots and find your faith in God again. I think you've seen that you don't have everything under control. Perhaps you've realized that you need Him to be in control. They can help you let go and let Him in again."

"Okay, Mom. I'll do it. It's a good idea." Drew was trying to stop crying, but she was overcome with emotion. Regret mingled with relief was a powerful emotion.

"As for today," Mr. Daniels said, "I have some things I want you to do around the house. Some yard work and some other projects that will keep you busy and give you time to think. Fair?"

"Fair," Drew agreed.

"One more thing, Drew." Her mom paused and collected her thoughts. "I don't want this conversation to end without making sure that you know how much your dad and I love you. This doesn't change that one bit. We love you so much that we aren't going to let you go down this path that you've found. We don't think you're a terrible person, and our love for you hasn't changed. We know that you've made some mistakes, and we're going to do our best to make sure it doesn't happen again."

Drew nodded as the tears fell hard on her lap.

"Also," Mrs. Daniels continued, "God's love for you hasn't changed a bit, either. He has begun a good work in your life; He began that work a long time ago. And the Bible promises in Philippians 1:6 that when He begins that good work in someone, He will carry it on to completion. He'll finish what He started in you. You just need to let go of the control and let Him be your Lord and Savior. You know what I mean?"

Drew nodded, still unable to talk. Her mom went to her immediately and put her motherly arms around her and held her until she could compose herself.

"I love you both. And I heard everything you said about letting God back into the driver's seat in my life. I will figure out how to do that. I want Him to finish His work in me."

The day passed quickly. Drew was surprised at how good it felt to work hard. She raked leaves, cleaned out the gutters, stacked wood, and organized the garage and the basement. She worked until she was sweating, and it was like a form of therapy. Dani helped her for a little while—not that Drew needed the help, but they needed the time together. As each project got completed, it felt like a piece of the broken puzzle of her life was put back together. Each time she moved on to the next project, she left a piece of the pain behind.

The one dark moment was when her dad came to tell her what had happened the night before, after they left. The police arrested everyone. Most of them got charged with underage drinking, others got charged with providing alcohol to minors or buying it with a fake ID. Several even got arrested for possession and/or use of drugs. Sorrow for her friends washed over her, but it was mingled, once again, with relief. Neither Drew nor her dad had any idea if this would mean jail time for any of them or if they would face suspension or expulsion from school. The fact that Drew could have easily been with them continued to fill her with immense relief even though she was so sad for her friends.

"Remember, Drew, real friends wouldn't have put you in a situation like that. They would have known that you weren't ready and that it was unsafe and illegal. Those types of kids aren't the kinds of friends you want. Do you realize that? Really?"

"Yeah, Dad. I mean, it's hard to let go of what I thought was a dream come true. But I see what you're saying and I agree. I miss my old friends. You know? Girls who made me a better person, made it easy to be who I am instead of making me work so hard to be who they wanted me to be."

"Ah, yes. I do think you get it, honey. That's exactly what I was hoping you'd realize." He gave her a little hug and then left her to finish her project.

Drew looked forward to going to church. She knew that she needed some spiritual healing. But she dreaded seeing the looks on people's faces and wondering if they knew the story. Oh well, she had to face everyone sooner or later.

Pastor Michaels was his usual fiery self. He was finishing up his series about control, and his sermon focused on how people need to let the attractive things of the world fade into the background rather than let them control desires and drive ambition.

"God doesn't value the things that the world does," Pastor Michaels taught. "Popularity, looks, human ability, and material things mean nothing to Him. In fact, the Bible tells us that people who want those things more than they want God's will already have their reward. That means that whatever you focus on is your reward. If your only goal is to get the most you can out of life, then your reward *is* this life. But if your goal is to love and serve God and you follow Him, then your reward comes from Him.

"The Bible says that where your heart is, there your treasure will be also. So, if your heart is set on the things of earth that fade and rust away, then you have shown Him where your treasure is. But if your heart is set on things above—God's will, showing His love to others, learning from and living the scriptures—then you will be showing God and the world where your treasure is. There is no mistaking it. You can't serve both God and the world.

"Just remember, all that glitters loses its luster in the light of God's glory. Let your heart and mind and all you desire be illuminated by the influence of God, not the temporary sparkle that the world offers."

Drew took in the words of the message that she felt was directed toward her. She decided once again that all that glittered was not what she wanted, and that He had everything under control.

My Decision

I, *(include your name here)*, have read the story of Drew Daniels and have learned from the choices that she made and the consequences that she faced. I promise to think before I act and, in all things, to choose God's will over mine. Specifically, I will honor my parents and avoid situations that include alcohol and drugs. I will also protect my purity by not sneaking around with boys and doing things that I have to hide from my parents.

Please pray the following prayer:

Father God, I know that I don't know everything, and I can't possibly have everything under control. Please help me remember the lessons I've learned as I've read this book. Help me to honor my parents and serve You by making right choices and avoiding questionable situations. It is my desire to avoid alcohol, drugs, and physical intimacy as I grow up. Help me to avoid situations that present those things as options to me. And if I find myself in a tight spot, please help me find a way out and give me the strength to take it. I know that You have everything under control, so I submit to Your will. Amen.

Congratulations on your decision! Please sign this contract signifying your commitment. Have someone you trust, like a parent or a pastor, witness your choice.

____

Signed

____

Witnessed by